SHOTGUN FREIGHTER

D1166460

SHOTGUN FREIGHTER

D. B. Newton

Chivers Press · G.K. Hall & Co.
Bath, England   Waterville, Maine USA

This Large Print edition is published by Chivers Press, England, and by G.K. Hall & Co., USA.

Published in 2002 in the U.K. by arrangement with the author c/o Golden West Literary Agency.

Published in 2002 in the U.S. by arrangement with Golden West Literary Agency.

U.K. Hardcover   ISBN 0–7540–4760–1 (Chivers Large Print)
U.K. Softcover   ISBN 0–7540–4761–X (Camden Large Print)
U.S. Softcover   ISBN 0–7838–9674–3 (Nightingale Series Edition)

The text of this Large Print edition is unabridged.
Other aspects of the book may vary from the original edition.

Set in 16 pt. New Times Roman.

Printed in Great Britain on acid-free paper.

British Library Cataloguing in Publication Data available

Library of Congress Cataloging-in-Publication Data

Newton, D. B. (Dwight Bennett), 1916–
    Shotgun freighter / D.B. Newton.
      p.   cm.
    ISBN 0–7838–9674–3 (lg. print : sc : alk. paper)
    1. Large type books. I. Title.
    PS3527.E9178 S56 2002
    813'.52—dc21
                            2001039969

CHAPTER ONE

The sound was little more than a hoarse echo, so out of place against the drab Kansas prairie that a man might easily not believe what he'd heard. Dan Rawley happened to have been listening for it, during the whole last hour of riding; but though he reined in the tired bay horse and waited for a repetition, it didn't come again. He decided some quirk of shifting autumn wind must have brought the sound to him, across that distance.

Changing position in saddle to stretch tired muscles, he turned as the assistant wagon boss rode alongside. 'You heard it, too?'

'Sure as hell did.' Hobie Drake was a big, weather-beaten man in his forties, with straw-yellow hair and a jaw like a shovel. Nodding, he said, 'That was a riverboat, whistling for the Bellport landing. Certainly tells a man he's home!'

Dan Rawley looked back along the line of the bull train, where the wind whipped dust in tawny sheets from beneath ponderously turning wheels. Canvas flapped like pistol shots, hanging slack on the hickory bows— these huge wagons, that had loaded three tons apiece for the Denver haul, were making the return trip empty and hitched tandem fashion, two or three to a team. This wasn't like the old

1

trade to Santa Fe; insatiable as the hunger for supplies might be at the Denver diggings, there was little enough as yet that needed hauling the other way. For that reason, a good many of the Kansas and Nebraska freighters actually counted their wagons and draft stock as part of the operating expense, to be disposed of at the end of each haul—even if it meant selling prime oxen for meat, or taking ten dollars for a fine Shuttler or Espenshied that had cost a couple hundred, new, at the wagon yard.

But Dan Rawley, among others, had proved to his own satisfaction that this was poor economics, and that it was well worth the trouble bringing the empty wagons back. His boss, Nate Archer, had needed some convincing; but in that, Nate only ran true to form. Both stubborn and vacillating by nature, he made problems for a wagon master—especially one like this Dan Rawley, who didn't respond well to interference.

Now, suddenly prodded by impatience, Dan Rawley turned again to ask Hobie Drake, 'Can you bring them on in without me?'

'Sure.' The assistant wagon boss gave him a shrewd look. 'I reckon you're anxious to get a bad thing over with . . .'

About to rein away, Dan Rawley paused. 'I don't think I know what you mean.'

'Why, you'll be breaking the news to Nate that you're quitting, won't you?'

2

'It's no news. I told him months ago.'

'I doubt he let it sink in much, because it's something he damn well wouldn't want to hear. I'll give you odds he puts up a hell of a squawk.'

The younger man frowned, but then he shrugged. 'Makes no difference. I did tell him.'

'You stand by that,' Hobie advised soberly. 'He's been riding your coattails long enough!'

Dan Rawley nodded, and lifted the bay out of the monotonous pace set by slowly plodding oxen.

In a matter of minutes the wagons had dropped from sight, in the gently rolling swells of this Eastern rim of Kansas. Presently then, the hills opened out and at the foot of a low bluff stretched the Missouri—a tawny expanse of water, turgidly flowing and eye-punishing where a smear of reflected sun turned it to bronze.

Scattered along the near bank lay the town. It was not as big as Atchison or Leavenworth, the rival ports downstream, but it drew its share of the River's trade. At the moment a couple of sternwheelers were tied up at the landing, while a third—no doubt, the one whose whistle he had heard—was just warping in on reversed engines and with bells jangling as she nosed to a berth, twin banners of smoke trailing from her stacks.

The arrival of a boat at one of these little River towns was an excitement that never flagged, for it gave to them the essential pulse of life. Dan Rawley could see tiny figures moving on deck and shore, now, as a rope was thrown over and the landing stage swung out. In another moment, barrels and crates would start their flow across and into the warehouses for storage, or directly into big freight rigs that were drawn up and waiting.

He rode down off the bluff with a feeling of coming home.

Along Water Street, the warehouses and the headquarters of the larger wagon freighters crowded the mud bank, with the town climbing the rise behind. Barely more than five years from its beginnings, this Bellport was raw enough—the dock crews and riverboat men, bullwhackers and muleskinners and the rest of the tough breed who followed the freighting business, brought violence with them but also a certain healthy vigor. The houses and business buildings that lined unpaved streets were ugly clapboard cubes, for the most part, though a few brick structures were beginning to make an appearance. In the residential section, young shade trees had even been planted which in a few years would mask the newness of everything and, hopefully, give it more a look of permanence.

Everywhere the dark, rank smell of the river bottom made its presence felt, insistently.

Dan rode directly to a place where a sprawl of sheds, stables, and other ramshackle

4

buildings formed a U-shaped compound, with not a blade of grass growing. In the open space of bare, packed dirt stood a couple of the big freight wagons; a corral held a tough-looking team of mules, chomping grain at the feed trough. As Dan Rawley dismounted, an old man in overalls came out of a barn carrying a pitchfork.

He was so bent with time and labor that his head was sunk permanently forward on his shoulders and he had to twist his neck and look at a person sidewise. He set the tines of his fork against the ground as he greeted Dan Rawley. 'Hey, Dan! You must have made good time. I wasn't looking for you.'

'We had us a good crossing,' Dan said, dismounting, favoring stiff muscles as he stepped to the ground. 'Both directions. No problems, except for the grass being about wiped out—travel on the Overland's been the heaviest this year that I've ever seen it.'

'What about the red beasties?'

'Not a sign of an Indian, going out—from Fort Kearney clear to Denver City. Heading back, there was a handful of Pawnees followed the train a way to see what they could beg or steal. When they decided the wagons were empty they didn't hang around long.' He added, 'Is Nate here?'

'In his office.' Charlie Clewes swung his hump-shouldered torso, to point with his chin in the direction of the ramshackle building.

'Want me to take care of the bay?'

Dan shook his head. 'I don't expect to stay long. And I'll be taking him with me.' He added, 'Drake's bringing in the wagons. They're maybe a half hour behind me.'

The old man nodded. Then, as the other started to turn away leading the horse, a sudden thought made him say, 'Maybe I should tell you. That damned Dutchman—that Cap Shulte . . .'

Dan halted, looking at him. 'What about Shulte?'

'He was in today. *And* yesterday, *and* the day before that. Each time, he was wanting to know if you was back or if we'd heard from you yet. I think there's something on his mind.'

The younger man's face settled into a stern coldness that took the warmth from the eyes and made them seem startlingly pale against the dark weathering of his skin. Dan Rawley said, 'He hasn't got a damn thing I'd be interested in hearing!'

'I didn't figure so. Just the same, maybe you better keep an eye open. Today he looked like he'd been drinking; and Shulte's the kind that likker turns mean. And if he wants what I think he does, it's something he's been nursing ever since you fired him off your wagons, at Fort Kearney a month ago.'

'He knows why I fired him.'

'I've heard his version. I was hoping you'd tell me what really happened.' Clewes slanted a shrewd look at the other. 'Reading between the lines, I sort of gather he got lit up on some of that Dobytown busthead, and put a bullet into an ox in his string that was giving him trouble.'

Dan returned the old fellow's look 'You read pretty good. It was the last straw. I'll have no such man working on a train that I boss. On the other hand, I'm not hunting for trouble with Cap Shulte—today, or any other.'

'You might not have to hunt for it,' Charlie Clewes suggested dryly. 'I'd watch my step, was I you—with him in town.'

Dan nodded. 'Thanks, oldtimer. I'll keep it in mind.' He turned and walked through winy October sunlight, toward the building that housed Nate Archer's headquarters. There he dropped the reins to anchor them, took down a pair of saddlebags from behind the cantle and slung them across an arm. He went up the steps.

In the ranks of the wagon freighters who operated out of Bellport and the other Missouri River towns, this Nate Archer didn't rate any great prominence. He'd had no experience himself on the trails, differing in this from his wagon master, Dan Rawley, who had served an early apprenticeship with the bull trains of the Santa Fe trade. Archer was a townsman, strictly—a small-scale merchant and businessman who'd seen the booming freighting business as a place to make a killing.

And he was still small-scale, as anyone could judge from the size of his wagonyard and of this cramped, untidy room that housed his office.

A thin-blooded man, he had kept a fire burning although it was not at all a cold day; the stuffy air reeked with the smell of the cheap cigars he favored. One lay fuming on the edge of a saucer that served him for an ashtray. As Dan entered, his boss looked up from behind the littered desk. With a grunt he laid aside his pen, pulled off gold-rimmed glasses and stuffed them into a pocket of his waistcoat.

Dan Rawley nodded greeting as he crossed the little room with its iron stove and wooden file cabinets and cheap office furnishings. He dropped his saddlebags onto a chair beside the desk, opened one and took from it an envelope. 'Made delivery of that shipment to Work & Mantley,' he said. 'Here's the receipt with Ed Mantley's signature, and a draft on their account. You can check the figures.'

Archer took the envelope, glanced quickly through its contents, nodded curtly. He tossed it on the desk and picked up his cigar. He was a man of uncertain age, gone bald now though his mutton chop whiskers were as luxuriant as they had ever been. He had a desk-worker's pallor and look of softness, and more than the beginning of a paunch; his black stare held a brooding discontent.

Leaning back, he put the cigar in his mouth and wheeled it with sensuous movements of his lips from one corner to the other.

'Another season done,' he muttered roughly. 'Just about.'

'And damned little to show for it! A man does well to meet his costs, let alone get anywhere in this business.'

Dan said nothing, but looking at his employer he was thinking this wasn't true. Between the Santa Fe and the gold fields, there was good money to be made in wagon freight these days, if a man was ambitious enough to go out and dig for it and wasn't afraid of a few risks. Even the turbulence along the Kansas–Missouri border—and all the talk of a victory for this fellow Lincoln and the Republicans in November maybe leading to secession and even war—couldn't keep the wagon trains off the roads, or lessen the clamor for merchandise that could reach those markets in no other way.

All it needed was that a man give half the concern to his business that he did to his own creature comforts. But nature hadn't made Nate Archer that kind of a man.

He asked now, 'You happen to hear anything from Frank Owen, while you were out there?'

Dan nodded. 'Ran into him in Denver. The store is doing well. Now he's thrown in with some other men and formed a company that has interests in a camp in California Gulch. They're pooling their capital and it sounds as though it could develop into something pretty good. At least he's optimistic.'

'Fine!' The other wagged his head. 'If it goes, that should mean more business next year, Daniel. Owen has been a good customer. Of course, I realize there's a special reason for that—almost a family reason, you might say.' He ran a palm across luxuriant side-whiskers as he slanted a look at the younger man. 'Long as you and Miss Vinnie Owen keep company, I guess there's not much danger of our losing the old man's account.' The corners of his mouth lifted in what served him for a smile. 'You just keep up the good work there!'

Dan Rawley's irritation, at this broad hint that brought a scowl and a stain of color to his dark face, was lost next instant in another thought. He said in a blunt tone, 'Wait just a minute! You haven't forgotten something, have you? What I told you back at the start of the season?'

The eyes, staring up into his own, narrowed slightly; the movement of the cigar between the flat lips was suddenly stilled. Too casually, Archer asked, 'And what would that have been?'

'That it was the last year I'd be working as your wagon boss. That I got other plans.'

Archer's expression showed nothing at all. Deliberately, he put up a hand and plucked

10

the cigar from his mouth, and looked at the burning end of it. 'Oh, yes. I do remember. There *was* something said, as to how you might—'

'It wasn't put that way, at all,' Dan corrected him. 'I gave you definite notice. Unless you happen to have something more lined up for me, I've just made my last haul for you, Nate. I finished out the season, as I promised. As of this moment, I'm no longer working for you.'

Nate Archer frowned. He rubbed his chin with the thumb of the hand that held his cigar, considering this as though it were an idea that had come to hit him unprepared. 'Daniel, I just don't understand,' he said finally. 'I always thought we got along.'

'I never claimed otherwise,' Dan Rawley answered patiently. There were certain things he could have brought up—an accumulation of irritations, in the three years he had worked for this man: all the petty finagling and cutting costs by using poor equipment and rundown stock, and hiring men of Cap Shulte's caliber for the wagon boss to deal with as best he could. But there was no point in raising such matters.

He found himself thinking, just now, of Hobie Drake's warning—that Archer wouldn't accept this without making a row. It began to look as though Hobie had been right.

The freighter put the cigar in his mouth and puffed at it angrily, scowling through the fog of

11

blue smoke that built in front of him. 'I suppose it's money you're holding out for,' he growled finally. 'Some other outfit's got to you, and has made you an offer you think I can't afford to match. I guess loyalty don't count for a damn any more!'

'Loyalty has nothing to do with this!' Dan snapped, beginning now to feel a stir of anger. 'I'm not leaving you to go with any other company, but simply because I want to make a start for myself. A man has that right, I guess.'

'For yourself?' the other echoed, staring at him. 'May I ask, what with? Who's backing you?'

'No one's backing me. I've managed to pile up a sort of a stake; I figure it will do for a start. I'll make it do.'

'I see.' The freighter leaned forward in his chair and angrily stubbed out his cigar. 'You'd walk out on a good job, for that—a piddling, poor-mouth operation, one man and a wagon and a spavined team and whatever you can find by hook or crook to haul with them! Just another damned shotgun freighter, by God!'

Dan said quietly, 'Call me that, if you like. I think I can make it.'

'And I think you can't!' Archer came to his feet. He was a few inches short of the other's spare height; he threw back his bald and bushy-whiskered head and peered at Dan with crackling anger in his stare. 'Why, you damned idiot! You'll fall on your face—and I just hope

12

you do! Leaving a man in the lurch—'

'I haven't left anyone in the lurch,' Dan said. 'I gave you almost a year's notice—plenty of time for you to find a new wagon boss. And if I'm an idiot, that's my affair. I just happen to be a man who'd rather be his own boss, even if he goes broke.' He added, 'So give me the wages that are due me for this final haul, and I'll be going.'

'Taking half my crew with you, I suppose?'

Patiently, Dan Rawley shook his head. 'You just said, yourself, a shotgun freighter can't afford a crew. Hobie Drake did mention something about wanting to throw in with me, but I told him it would have to be cleared with you. I got no wish to hurt your business in any way, Nate.'

Archer gave a snort. 'Drake? Who needs him? Or any other bastard that would walk out on a man! The hell with him! The hell with both of you!' His whole face twisted in a grimace of pure meanness.

Dan looked at this man who had been his boss for three years. There was no sense in matching his resentments; he held back the retort he might have made, and said nothing more than, 'Have it your way, Nate. You will anyhow.' A moment later, saddlebags over his shoulder and his money in his pocket, Dan Rawley walked out of there into the cleaner, better smelling air of the autumn day.

He felt almost like a man stepping from

unpleasant bondage into freedom.

CHAPTER TWO

Since Hobie Drake could perfectly well finish bringing the wagons in, Dan Rawley felt justified in walking away from a job that had taken most of his waking hours and conscious thought for the past three years. It was a moment he had long looked forward to; all that spoiled it was Nate Archer's unreasonable nature.

As far as he could see, he'd been perfectly fair and above board. Still, he had to remember Hobie Drake had warned him Nate wouldn't like admitting he had to let Dan go. Archer was a difficult man—as Dan Rawley had as good reason as anyone to know.

The freight yard lay at the northern edge of town. Mounting again, he rode through streets sparsely lined with cottonwoods and locusts from which colored leaves were falling, a smell of burning leaves tanging the autumn afternoon. Having left his horse at a livery stable he went directly to his boardinghouse. The room that was his home was plain enough, furnished with a brass bed, a rocker and a straight chair, a dresser, a wardrobe. It was musty and close-smelling after being shut up for nearly two months.

Dan ran the window open and propped it with a stick. He had ordered hot water and a tub sent up; he stripped and enjoyed his first leisurely soaking since the hotel in Denver City, then shaved and dressed in the luxury of clean clothes. Cheeks stinging to the pull of the razor through tough beard, he looked at his reflection in the flawed mirror and had to grin ruefully at what he saw—the blunt, broad-cheeked face, weather-whipped to bronze almost as dark as an Indian's, contrasted oddly with the blue eyes and the sharp line of pallor drawn across his forehead by his hat brim. He smoothed back the thick brown hair with both palms; and having polished his boots a trifle, he drew on his flat-crowned, broad-brimmed hat and set out upon his second call on this afternoon of his arrival.

The Owen place was no mansion, but it was a prosperous one for this Kansas riverfront town. The house, like the town, was less than six years old—Frank Owen had brought his family here from Illinois when Kansas Territory was first opened, selecting this particular location because he saw Bellport as a place with a future—a good place for a merchant to establish himself. The size of his house showed that he had prospered.

Actually, it was rather too large now, for Owen's wife had died the year before, taken quite suddenly by illness. The house was white, two-storied, with tall, narrow windows and

15

doors, and scrollwork dripping from the pointed eaves and the edges of the porch roof. It sat by itself, behind a picket fence, with an iron stag in the lawn.

Dan twisted the bell knob. After a moment, the big door was opened hesitantly by a black woman whose careful look was that of a free Negro who knew there were many white men, both here in this Kansas Territory and across the River in Missouri, who felt she had no right to be anything but a chattel slave. At sight of the caller, her caution melted instantly in a smile that showed all her dazzling array of teeth, and she flung the door wide. 'Why, Mistuh Rawley! We never knows when to look for you. I hopes I sees you well?' she added, as he stepped in and she took his hat and closed the door.

'Couldn't be better, Sarah,' Dan assured her. 'Is anyone home?'

'You means Miss Vinnie, of course. You go right on into the parlor, Mistuh Rawley. I'll tell her she got company. You'll be staying to supper, I reckon?'

He pointed out, 'I haven't been asked . . .'

'You'll be staying,' she concluded, with a knowing nod of the head. 'I'll set the extra place . . .'

She took her portly shape down the hallway, and Dan Rawley turned through a wide archway into the parlor to the left, with its flowered carpet and maroon drapes and good,

16

solid furniture in plush and dark mahoganies.

A tall, well-dressed man stood with his back to the cold fireplace. He was reading a newspaper and he lifted a glance as Dan entered. The trim black beard and mustache, together with a hint of gray at the temples, made him look somewhat older than he was; so, too, did the almost sullen cast of his lean features. Wes Boyd actually was in his middle thirties, only a few years Dan Rawley's senior. The rest was illusion, compacted of a certain cynicism and an air of impatient boredom. One who didn't know him might have judged that a hard life had disappointed this man. It was Dan Rawley's secret opinion that he was merely spoiled.

He was Frank Owen's nephew, treated like a true son and placed in full charge of the merchant's affairs in Bellport, now that Owen himself was looking to his new store and his mining investments in the Denver area. He performed his duties well enough, but Dan couldn't see that they felt any real interest in him. Now he returned Dan's greeting with little more than a grunt and an indifferent nod, apparently not caring enough to ask about his latest trip, the condition of the crossing, or what word there might have been in Denver as to his uncle's affairs there.

This was wholly typical, and Dan refused to let it bother him. Instead, he indicated the paper in Boyd's hands as he asked, 'What's the news?'

'More of the same,' the other said with a shrug. 'More boring talk about the South pulling out if that baboon, Lincoln, should happen to be elected. A man gets damned sick and tired of listening to it.'

Dan Rawley frowned, deciding to pass over the insult to a man for whom he was beginning to feel considerable respect. 'You don't think they'll go through with it? You don't think they'll secede?'

'They haven't got the guts,' Wes Boyd answered scornfully. 'And if they did, what could Lincoln do about it?'

'He could fight.'

Boyd folded the paper. 'There'll be no war,' he stated with positive assurance. 'Obviously it's the last thing anybody wants.'

'We've had war here in Kansas Territory for the past five years,' Dan reminded him. 'A war nobody wanted . . .'

Wes Boyd didn't like to be contradicted. His head lifted and he stabbed a cold, sideward look at the other. 'That,' he said flatly, slapping the folded newspaper against a palm, 'was a different matter.'

'Was it?'

Dan was thinking of certain things he'd seen on the trail—burned cabins, crops that had been deliberately destroyed. Once, even, a man hanging dead, his face blackened by the sun and distorted by the slow agony of

18

strangulation—and no way to know whether it had been the work of pro-slavery Border Ruffians from over Missouri way, or the equally bloodthirsty men of the other camp: Jim Lane and his Redlegs, or even Osawatomie Brown who last year had died on the scaffold for his raid on the arsenal at Harper's Ferry in Virginia.

But, perhaps, for Boyd none of this really counted.

Bellport, in its rather favored location here on the River, in this northeast corner of the Territory, had missed the real agony of Bleeding Kansas; it had known only rumors of the turmoil and horror of Lawrence and the Wakarusa. So long as it stayed away from his own door, it was all no doubt as uninteresting to Wes Boyd as he now found the prospect of a great nation threatening to split apart and become engulfed in the same madness.

Something that might have led into argument came to an abrupt halt then, as a quick tapping of heels and a swirl of skirts brought Vinnie Owen into the room, and drove all thought of quarreling from Dan's mind. At his turn she halted an instant in the archway, as though some remembered decorum warned her she should make a proper entrance: but then she was coming straight at him, her hands outstretched and her whole face ashine with welcome. As he took her hands, Dan heard a snort of amusement from Wes Boyd. Neither paid the man any notice, and a moment later a door closed quietly as he discreetly withdrew.

Lavinia Owen was just twenty. She was not a tall girl, and taffy-colored curls brushed her shoulders as she looked up at Dan Rawley. Gray eyes sparkled; a voice that was breathy with excitement cried, 'Dan! I've been thinking so much about you!'

'Me, too. All the way from Denver . . .'

Suddenly he drew her to him, an arm encircling her shoulders, the other reaching for her waist. He heard her quick gasp, then he bent and his mouth trapped hers and he kissed her soundly. When he let her go she stumbled back and her eyes were wide, her cheeks flaming.

'And I been thinking about *that* all the way, too,' he said bluntly. 'Wondering if I'd find the nerve to try it!'

Her hands pressed against her cheeks; her eyes held astonishment. 'You have no cause to complain of your nerve, Dan Rawley!' But he could tell she was a good deal short of anger, and a warm pleasure flowed through him.

'I've brought you something from your father.' He took it from his pocket, a bulky envelope. 'I think it's a diary Frank's been keeping for you—he asked if I'd fetch it along, and of course I was glad to.'

'Oh, thank you, Dan!' She took it from him, delighted. But when she saw her name on the envelope, in her father's bold scrawl, she became very quiet and he was sure she was fighting back a sudden smarting of tears. 'Oh, Dan! I miss him so! The house seems so empty, with him gone—no one home but Wes, and me, and Sarah . . .'

'Go ahead and read it,' he offered. 'I won't mind.'

'No.' She placed the envelope on a mahogany table that held a beaded runner and some flowers under a glass bowl. 'I'll save it for when I'm alone. Right now there's too much to talk about.'

Apparently the kiss was forgiven, though not likely to be forgotten. It lay between them during a long and trembling moment, serving to silence them both. Then Vinnie said, 'You're staying for supper, aren't you?'

A slow grin warmed his face. 'Sarah already gave me orders about that,' he told her. 'So I guess I'm staying, all right.'

The room where they ate, like the rest of this house, reflected a prosperous merchant's attempt at elegance and tradition in a raw, new place. As early dusk settled outside the high windows, lamplight glistened on cut glass and on heavy silver service that had belonged to Vinnie's mother. Dan suspected that Sarah had set the table with the best they had, to make an impression on this tall, bronzed man of whom she thoroughly approved.

For his part, he had come here strictly to see

Franklin Owen's daughter. Though Sarah's chicken pie with dumplings was delicious, he would scarcely have noticed if he had been eating it off a tin plate—which was a style he was well accustomed to after countless meals squatting beside a wagon camp cookfire, out on the trails.

Wes Boyd sat in silence at his end of the table, speaking seldom and answering Dan's few polite questions about the mercantile business so curtly that Dan soon gave up trying to make conversation and left the man to himself. And very shortly Boyd finished his meal and walked out, mumbling an excuse. Moments later the big front door closed.

Vinnie's brow puckered as she looked after her cousin. 'He certainly wasn't very civil, was he?' she exclaimed indignantly.

Dan shrugged 'What of it? He does his job, I guess—managing things at home, so your pa can see to his interests in the gold fields. No law says he has to go out of his way just to be pleasant to me.'

'All the same! He lives in this house. You're a guest, and at least should be treated like one.' She shook her head. 'He's so moody! I've known him all my life, and yet sometimes I wonder if I really know him at all.'

But Dan hadn't come here to discuss Wes Boyd. In a moment, now that they were alone, he was telling her his own news: 'I gave notice, today. I'm no longer on Archer's payroll.'

She was pleased. 'Then you've really done it! Oh, I'm glad, Dan. That man has worked you too hard!'

'As for that,' he said dryly, 'if I was afraid of working, I'd be in some other business. And now I'm on my own, I suppose I'll find out what work really is.'

'But at last you'll be accomplishing something. You've carried Nate Archer long enough!'

'At any rate, after this if I stand or fall I've got no one else to share the credit, or the blame . . .'

She wanted to know his plans and they sat a long time, discussing them. 'Hobie Drake wants to go into the thing with me,' Dan said. 'And I'd be a fool not to let him, even though he hasn't any capital. He's a good man, and I've got enough saved for a start. Everything depends on our being able to make at least one run out to the mountains before winter sets in—two, if we can manage.'

Vinnie stared at him. 'But, it's October already! You can't possibly hope to—'

'We not only can, but on this kind of a shoestring we have to. This will be fast freight—no bull train. We'll use mules and a single wagon. We carry our feed, and load light with the kind of thing I know I can dispose of at a good profit. Perishables, that sort of thing. By spring, when the grass is up, we should be ready for a real operation.'

23

She was looking at his eyes, her own expression sober. 'Dan, I know you'll make it. You're going to be a big man in this Territory!'

'I wouldn't say that—but at least I'll be my own man. And I guess I'm just stubborn enough, I have to have it that way or none!'

'Whatever it is you want, you know I want it for you. But—' Her eyes became troubled. 'I can't help wondering: The turmoil around us, and the papers full of talk about secession— maybe even war! What's it going to do to all of us?'

'I don't know,' he answered soberly. 'But until it happens, we can't let it interfere. There'll always be trouble of some kind. We'll simply go ahead and hope for the best. And if *this* trouble comes we'll try to take it in stride.'

It was still early when he said good night— he was bone-weary from the saddle, and all his days from now on would be busy ones. A harvest moon had risen and when they stepped out onto the deep veranda it hung golden above the Missouri rim, flooding this river town with its mellow glow, softening the harshness of the land. They stood for a long moment, absorbing it.

'Well—' Dan Rawley said, finally, and then let the speech die because it was not a time for words. They turned and looked at each other; and this time, when they came together, there was no awkward clumsiness, no self-conscious embarrassment to their embrace. Vinnie's whole face seemed to shine with the rich soft light, and then her arms were tight about his neck as their lips met.

As he released her, she said quietly, 'Good luck, Dan.'

'You're my luck, Vinnie,' he told her. And he really believed it.

CHAPTER THREE

Hobie Drake, like his friend Dan Rawley, had a social call planned that evening. It was one he had been looking forward to with considerable anticipation, though neither Dan nor anyone else knew anything about it. Of his personal affairs—in any matter very close to his feelings—Hobie was not a man to do much talking.

First he completed his duties in connection with bringing in this bull train. The empty wagons had to be hauled to Nate Archer's freight yard and lined neatly inside the fence, the teams unspanned, the yokes carefully stacked and the draft oxen driven out to a flat stretch of prairie beyond the edge of town, until Archer decided what he wanted done with them. It was close to sundown when all this had been completed, and Hobie stopped to talk gossip for a moment with Charlie Clewes, and call his attention to a weakened

25

axle on one of the big wagons. He had been watching it carefully during the last hundred miles of the journey, but it had held up.

Afterward, carrying his single-load Sharps rifle and the canvas bag containing his bedroll and other belongings, he started across the yard from the stables—and found Nate Archer standing in the doorway of his office, waiting.

Hobie would as soon have walked on by, as though not noticing. He had no liking for his employer and felt he did a better job of it, the fewer personal dealings they had. But Archer apparently had other ideas at the moment. He called Hobie's name, sharply, and the latter made a face and halted as the man came toward him.

Archer had left his hat inside, and the last of the sunlight made his bare scalp gleam as though he kept it polished. Too bad, Hobie Drake often thought, that he couldn't have kept some of that hair on his head, and not let it go to waste in those ridiculous mutton chop whiskers. He came to a stand and said, without preliminary, 'I suppose you know that sonofabitch Rawley just walked out on me!'

Hobie chose his words with care. 'I knew Dan told you, way last spring, this was the last season he'd be working for you.'

That earned him a stabbing glance from the narrowed black eyes, a tightening of the thin lips. 'Some men,' the freighter muttered savagely, 'have no sense of gratitude or obligation. When I think of all I've done for the bastard!' Hobie blinked, but otherwise managed to keep a straight face. Apparently Nate had been sitting in that pigsty of an office, brooding and constructing a fantasy that satisfied him. Now he went on: 'Well— we'll see! Without my backing, he'll fall on his face and be back asking to be taken on again. Maybe I'll bother to make a place for him, and maybe I won't!

'You were going to say something?' he added sharply, as Hobie Drake's lips moved.

'Yeah.' The yellow-haired man had heard enough. He spoke with studied bluntness, angered past diplomacy. 'I was gonna say that I been figuring I just might throw in with Dan. I thought, one of these days, I might be in to see you and draw the pay I got coming. But now, I reckon I won't wait. I'll take it now!'

Nate Archer bobbed his head, in angry satisfaction. 'Uh-huh. That's just about what I could have expected, after something Rawley let drop. Well, I don't need your kind either. You can have your money—and then, get out of my sight!' He had it ready, it seemed; he was digging in a pocket of his waistcoat and he brought out three twenty-dollar gold pieces. They glittered in fading sunlight as he flung them into the dirt at Hobie Drake's feet, and turned to walk away.

Hobie looked at the coins lying in the dirt, and his face flooded with crimson. He took a

27

quick stride then. His unencumbered right hand caught Archer by a shoulder and spun him around, and then he very deliberately gathered a fistful of Archer's clothing and dragged the man to him. He loomed a good six inches the taller. With no effort, he pulled Archer up on the toes of his polished boots, and thrust his prominent jaw into the other's face.

'When I've earned my pay,' he said evenly, 'I like it handed to me respectful. Now, suppose you pick it up and try again.'

Nate Archer swore and batted at the hand that held him prisoner. Hobie Drake simply gave the handful of clothing a further twist, forcing the other's head back and cutting off his wind. Archer was sweating suddenly and his face began to lose color. Hobie held him like that an instant longer, then with a downward sweep of his arm literally drove Archer to his knees. There he released the man, and stood waiting. Archer, gagging and choking for breath, knelt in the dirt with head hanging. A shudder went through him, visibly. Still on his knees, he scooped up the three gold eagles. When he stumbled to his feet, his face was white with fury. A hot, hating look stabbed Hobie Drake; he flung the coins into the hand Hobie held out for them, and the latter said calmly, 'Thanks.'

The freighter whirled and made for his office, and Hobie watched him go—not feeling any pleasure in humiliating a man, simply judging he had got his own. In the door of the stable he could see Charlie Clewes bobbing his head and grinning with real approval. Hobie merely pocketed his money and walked out of the freight yard.

Now that he had his pay he proceeded to get rid of some of it, going first to an outfitter's where he bought himself everything new, from the skin out. Carrying his packages into the backroom of a barber shop across the street, he discarded the filthy wreckage of the clothes that had seen him over the trail. After a pleasant session in the tin tub, he stood on spongy duckboards while he donned his new apparel—a white shirt with wide blue stripes, an off-orange ready-made suit whose trousers showed three horizontal creases from lying stacked on the merchant's shelf. Hobie stuck his tie and stiff collar into a pocket, for the time being, and went out into the shop to let the barber trim his yellow mane back from his ears and put the razor to his tangled beard.

The result left his bony, weathered face oddly patched, the pallor of jowls and back of neck contrasting with the deep, raw redness where cheeks and brow, below the customary line of his hat brim, had been exposed to the full beat of the sun. As he finished a tall yarn with which he'd been entertaining the barber and a set of grinning customers, Hobie hooked his collar in place and awkwardly fashioned something out of the bright flowered four-in-hand. He set his new, broad-brimmed and low-crowned hat carefully in place, and left the shop wafting the scent of the toilet-water the barber had liberally doused him with.

Ten minutes later he was seated at a table in the hotel dining room, napkin tucked into shirt collar, when Meg Crocker came in from the kitchen with her arms filled with steaming platters. Hobie caught her eye and grinned, getting a surprised stare in answer. When she had served the other customers, Meg came to him, showing her pleasure only in her smile and the warm sparkle of her brown eyes.

She was a woman in her early forties, going a little to weight, with an ample bosom and a good and generous face under gray-streaked brown hair. Hobie Drake, who knew her story, understood the spirit and courage of this woman—a widow, with a pair of youngsters dependent on her. He liked the kids, and he admired the mother. He nodded and said, 'Evening, Meg.'

'Mister Drake!' Good friends as they had become, she still addressed him formally even when they were alone. 'I've been watching your table these last few evenings. Been hoping you hadn't run into any trouble . . .'

'Me? Not a chance!' he assured her carelessly. His grin widened and he added, 'You're looking good.'

A trifle flustered, she raised a plump hand

to her hair to make sure nothing was out of place. 'It's not right to flatter an old woman like that!'

'Heck, now! You ain't so old. Anyhow, I'm gettin' a little long in the tooth my own self . . . How are the youngsters?'

'Just fine and dandy.'

'I brought a little something for 'em from Denver City. For you too, Meg. How soon can I see you?'

'I'm off at the usual time.'

He wagged his bony head. 'Gives me a chance to grab some supper first. You know what's in the kitchen—bring on whatever looks good.' She smiled, nodding, and left him to return presently with a plate of beef stew and biscuits and a cup of steaming coffee.

Hobie fell to with a will. When it came to efficient, enthusiastic eating, few men could match him. Customers who had already been served before he entered were still busy over their plates when he wiped up the last of his gravy with bread, finished off a slab of dried apple pie in three stabs of the fork, and washed it all down with a third cup of coffee. Unhooking his napkin with a sigh of contented repletion, he left money for his meal and walked out of the dining room and into the early evening, with a good part of an hour still left to kill before it would be time to return and pick up Meg Crocker and escort her home.

There were the expensive saloons, like the Bellport House: but Hobie considered these well out of his class. Instead, he gravitated by natural attraction to the dives along lusty, brawling Water Street, where the kind of men he liked and understood could generally be found—the deck crews and stevedores from the steamboat landing, the muleskinners and the tough bull-train men, the occasional enlisted man from Fort Leavenworth some twenty miles down river.

His own favorite haunt was Milligan's, a gambling hall and saloon run by a hard-fisted Irishman who had made a stake in the rough-and-tumble of the Santa Fe, but now considered himself too old and beat-up for the hardships of the long trails. Here Hobie could always be sure of a friendly welcome and a drink in relaxing company—and if he felt like it, a chance to lose his wages on faro, roulette and black-jack layouts that were scrupulously and honestly run.

Tonight he settled for a single drink from Milligan's best stock, to cut the long thirst of the trail from Denver City. He took it standing at the cherrywood bar, exchanging greetings with his friends and admiring the forthright naturalism of Milligan's art work. Early as it was, some of the games were already going. Presently, curiosity brought Hobie Drake's idle attention to a poker table in a near corner of the large, high-ceilinged room, because two of the men involved there seemed out of place in Milligan's.

They both appeared too well dressed, for one thing—especially the one, a stranger, who sat facing him. The cut of his clothes was sharp, there was a chain of gold nuggets across his flowered waistcoat, and a brilliant red jewel of some sort winking from the flowing cravat. To Hobie Drake the stone, like everything else about the man, looked phony. Tall and narrow-shouldered, he had pinched features and a sweeping moustache, pouches under his eyes, a bad complexion that suggested his skin seldom saw daylight. The deft movements of his hands, as he pulled in a pot and stacked the chips, reminded Hobie of the kind of professional card shark he had seen working the saloons of the river packets.

He wondered if Milligan knew or approved that such a man was working his tables. Personally he thought he'd never be caught dead sitting in a game with him.

The second one, seated opposite, puzzled him even more. He presented only a partial profile to Hobie but the latter was intrigued, thinking for some reason he should recognize the man, who had lost heavily on the hand now and threw his cards onto the table with an angry gesture. And as he turned to catch a waiter's eye and bark an order for drinks, Hobie saw his face and realized it was Wes Boyd—the relative who managed Frank

Owen's affairs here in Bellport, while Frank was busy at Denver City.

Somehow, this bothered Hobie. A dive like Milligan's was all right for a roughneck like him, but it was a strange place to see a member of the Owen family. Stranger, still, to see the man involved in gambling with a raffish tinhorn; why couldn't he stay in his own class, at the Territorial Club up on the hill, for instance? And why couldn't he pick better gambling partners? Hobie thought, 'If I was Frank Owen I wouldn't want to put too much trust in a man who plays poker in Water Street dives —and loses!'

Well, it was no concern of his, though he resolved he'd make some mention of this to Dan Rawley when he saw his friend again. Just now it was time for him to be getting back to the hotel. He turned down a drink that Milligan offered him on the house, took a rain check on it instead. Not long afterward he was ensconced in a chair on the hotel veranda when Meg Crocker emerged, off-duty and ready to start home. Hobie stood and took one plump elbow.

Walking beside her, through this tough town that was beginning to tune up as night settled, he plunged into an amusing account of his trip West. Meg was a good listener, which served as a necessary balm to Hobie Drake's ego. He enlarged a bit on the incidents of a haul that had actually been more or less routine, and discreetly toned down some of his more disreputable activities in Denver City. He told her about the things he had in his coat pocket for the youngsters—some real Cheyenne arrowheads for Bud, a string of glass beads for Susie. Meg's own present, a Mexican scarf for which he knew he'd paid entirely too much, he saved for a better moment when he could give it to her in private.

He also refrained from saying anything, yet, about his breakup with Nate Archer. He had an idea how she would react to that. Because of the hardships and uncertainties of her own life, Meg Crocker would surely have been alarmed at the thought of his giving up the security of steady pay. Hobie for his part was serenely confident he could get as good a job or better, any day or any place he wanted to look for it; but he knew Meg would worry, and kept quiet. Plenty of time to tell her later.

There was a disturbance. In one of the town's saloons, right beside them, angry voices burst into sudden excited yelling. Boots tromped floorboards, and a blow landed, and a man came spilling backward through the open door. He caught at a porch pillar to keep from going down in a sprawl, turning as another man lunged after him. They came together with a smash; they stood toe to toe, and blows were traded as onlookers jammed the doorway. And out of the general uproar emerged a meaningful phrase or two, to stab like a knife at a man's startled awareness: *'Goddam stinkin' Abolitionist...'*

Hobie and the woman had halted when the violence broke out, almost on top of them. Now he said roughly, 'Let's get out of this!' Meg didn't seem to hear. She stared transfixed, and when he touched her arm he could feel the locked and frozen stiffness that held her, every tendon and muscle strung taut. Hobie looked at her in alarm and a tar-barrel flare showed him the wide-eyed terror in a face gone deathly pale.

He didn't hesitate. At that instant the fight came spilling down off the saloon porch. Hobie Drake stepped forward and caught one combatant before he could back-pedal into them, a hand closing down hard on his shoulder and holding him like a vise. He swung the man around and as the second came swarming down the steps after him, Hobie grabbed that one by his coat collar. 'Quit this!' he roared. And as though it cost him no effort whatever, he brought the two of them together, their skulls colliding with a solid crunch of flesh and bone. Afterward, when he thrust them away, one man spun and fell headlong in the dirt of the street, where he lay motionless; the other staggered back against the porch rail and hung there dazed, staring at Hobie, blood running down his face.

Everything stopped. Into the gaping stillness of the suddenly quieted group in the doorway,

Hobie said sternly, 'Damn it, you got no respect for a lady? Next time, keep your brawlin' inside the saloons and off the public thoroughfare!' Dismissing them all, he took Meg Crocker's arm firmly in his big hand. 'They won't bother you now, ma'am.' They passed on, a dozen turning heads following them in a silence unbroken except for the tread of Hobie's cowhide boots on the plankings.

As soon as all that was left behind them, Hobie Drake stopped and turned anxiously to his companion. 'Meg?' he said. 'Old girl, you all right?' She seemed to sway; suddenly she dropped her face into her hands, and when he placed an arm about her shoulders he could feel the trembling and the sobs of near hysteria that racked her. 'Now, now!' he said in a tone of—for him—surprising gentleness.

In just a moment she got control of herself. Wiping wet cheeks with the palms of her hands, she said faintly, 'I'm sorry.'

'It's all right. I know . . .'

Surely no one could have blamed Meg Crocker, if they knew her story. For her and her husband, Bleeding Kansas had been something much more than a scarehead in a newspaper. Sam Crocker had never owned a slave, nor wanted to; he'd brought his wife and kids out of Missouri, searching for a bit of free land in the new Territory, and he'd settled among other, friendly Missourians in that bloody southeast sector near Fort Scott. He was too busy working his homestead claim to be bothered with politics. But that hadn't made any difference when the free-soil men—led, some declared, by old Osawatomie Brown himself—came rampaging along the creek bottoms, hunting out their enemies. Sam Crocker had been marched away with the rest and at daylight Meg had ventured out and found him in the heap of bodies, shot three times and butchered as he lay bleeding to death.

It wasn't an experience that a sensitive woman recovered from completely, even after three years, but she had stood up well. She was making a life for herself and her children, and doing a brave job of it. Still, she had watched the clouds of violence that had engulfed her family settling deeper over Kansas, and an outburst like this one tonight was enough to rouse all the buried terrors that would never be completely stifled.

Her hands clutched at Hobie; her eyes, big and tragic in the care-worn but still handsome face, searched for his own. 'Why can't they leave people alone?' she cried hoarsely. 'Those Abolitionists! They killed Sam—isn't that enough for them, without trying to start a war?'

Hobie Drake frowned. It was one subject they couldn't talk about. He came from Illinois, himself, and he had strong feelings on the subject of the Union and slavery. Here in Kansas, on one occasion, he'd actually helped to courier a batch of runaways along the underground railway into Iowa; but this was something he had never told Meg Crocker, nor would he argue with her now. He patted her shoulder as he murmured, 'Sho', now. Nobody's hurting you, old girl. Nobody! You understand? Neither you, nor the kids—not while I'm around.'

He saw her manage a tremulous smile. Her own hand came up, clutched his tightly. 'You're good, Hobie Drake. You're good and kind. I hope you don't mind how shamelessly I lean on you!'

'Sho' now.' He grinned. 'A man takes to a certain amount of leanin' on. Didn't you know? Now come along.' He tucked her hand into the crook of his elbow. Her fingers were still cold to the touch, and he covered them with his own huge paw as he walked her homeward to her children, through the spreading glow of a harvest moon.

CHAPTER FOUR

Dan Rawley, returning to his rooming house, had paused a moment before the bright splash of fight and sound that was the Bellport House, while he debated whether he had energy enough to step inside, or should go straight home. In there, he knew, would be friends, good whisky to help ease the tiredness from his shoulders, likely a profitable exchange of news.

Yet he decided, on reflection, he was really wearier than he'd thought; and, once a man got with friends it wasn't always easy to get away from them. Just now a soft bed seemed far more welcome. So he turned to pass on—and had his pleasant lethargy jarred out of him by the voice that spoke suddenly at his back, a voice that was heavy with malice and blurred with drink: 'You! Yeah—you, mister! Turn around here, and let me see you!'

Dan Rawley tensed, then settled his shoulders in a mood of resigned acceptance. He had known it was a moment he had to face, sooner or later, but it was the last thing he'd wanted tonight. His nerves were strung taut as he came slowly about to confront the high and wide shape of the man who stood, half visible, in the shadows piled deep and black on this eastern side of the street. Golden moonglow brought out the faint glimmer of his face, and of forearms bared by sleeves rolled above the elbow. It touched glints from the buckle of a belt, and the metal of the Navy Colt thrust behind it.

There was a sharp intake of breath. 'By God, it is!' Cap Shulte exclaimed. 'It really is! Rawley, I been looking for you to show—I

40

been looking so long, I damn near give up waiting!'

Dan Rawley kept his voice flat and without emotion. 'I was told you'd been asking about me.'

'You goddamned right! We got unfinished business to settle!'

'I don't think so. You know why you were fired. When I left you at Kearney, I made it clear I never wanted to cross trails with you again.'

One of those thick forearms lifted as the Dutchman stabbed a pointing finger. 'You done to me what nobody else ever dared to try! You left me stranded in the middle of nowhere!'

'I see you got back all right.'

Shulte's voice, carrying a recognizable freight of whisky anger, grew louder and even uglier. 'I suppose you ain't been talking big, all the way from here to Denver City, about how you went and kicked Cap Shulte off your goddamned wagon train!'

'If anyone's been talking,' Dan replied, levelly, 'it wasn't me. *You're* the one doesn't seem able to leave it alone—though I can't understand why you'd want it advertised that I had to fire you for going out of your head and destroying a good draft animal . . .'

With a roar almost like an animal's, the big man came at Dan—a long stride, that made the boards of the walk sag under the heavy

41

boot—and Shulte's right hand pawed at his waistcoat and came away holding gunmetal. Dan caught his breath as the barrel settled upon his chest; his own hands started to lift, then dropped again and he felt the sweat leak out.

He looked at the gun and then up at the face that he couldn't really see in this half light. He wished he could read the look of the slightly bulging, steely blue eyes, and the mouth under its bush of sandy mustache. He could smell the whisky on the man, but that was normal with Cap Shulte—it didn't tell him whether the man was actually drunk beyond reason, as he'd been that day at Kearney.

Dan swallowed, and fought to keep any tremor of fear out of his voice. 'It's murder if you use that!' he said sharply. 'I'm not armed.'

Shulte cursed him, viciously. The gun in his hand lifted a trifle and Dan Rawley knew with sick certainty that in another moment the big fellow was either going to shoot it, or use the barrel as a club. He tensed, trying to decide on a move if it were humanly possible—and at that moment, unexpectedly, a voice broke in on them, calling his name.

Unnoticed by either, a man had been crossing the street toward them, at an angle from the opposite wall. Now he must have decided he recognized Dan Rawley in the half light, for he paused as he said, 'That *is* you, isn't it, Dan? I thought it looked like—'

42

The interruption, slight as it was, had unsettled Cap Shulte's attention if only for an instant, and Dan Rawley took what advantage from it he could. Instead of trying to duck away from the menace of the gun, a useless maneuver, he waded right into it. A forearm, rising, struck the barrel upward and away; his shoulder took Cap Shulte in the chest and pulled him back against the wall of the building.

Shulte cried out but was unable to avoid the impact. As they collided, the breath rushed from his lungs, freighted with whisky fumes. Then Shulte's thick shoulders slammed against siding and his thumb was jarred off the hammer flange. The gun went off, a shocking rush of sound. The spurt of muzzle fire lit both their faces briefly, lighting twin flares in the Dutchman's staring blue eyes and glinting whitely from bared, clenched teeth.

But Dan had his gunwrist trapped against the wall and now, with a quick shift, he caught the hand that held the gun and twisted, hard. Shulte couldn't hold onto the weapon. It came away in Dan's grasp, and he stepped back as he transferred it hastily to his right hand.

'Cool down!' Dan warned. 'Don't make me use this!'

Shulte went still; Dan moved cautiously away, keeping the man covered with his own gun. He was aware of excited voices stammering questions, roused by sound of the shot. But he knew they would quiet down quickly enough when it wasn't repeated. Even here, in the better part of town, such things were taken pretty much for granted. For himself, he suddenly realized he was trembling and that the mild autumn night felt icy cold to his sweat-soaked clothing.

George Byam, the man whose interruption had given Dan Rawley his chance to turn the tables, had forgotten to move. He stood precisely as he had when he spoke, and now he found his voice again and it was husky with shock. 'For the love of God! What's going on here?'

'It's all over,' Dan Rawley said across his shoulder. Still keeping that captured Navy Colt trained on the big man, he told Shulte firmly, 'I'm not going to put up with any more of this. We had a difference, and you built it out of all proportion. Now, keep clear of me—you understand?'

He waited for an answer, but Shulte merely glared in hating silence. Dan shrugged and started to turn away, and it was then that the man forced out grudging speech. 'What about my gun?'

Dan hesitated. He nodded toward the brightly lighted entrance of the Bellport House, where a half dozen customers had gathered to learn what was going on in the street. 'I'll leave it for you there, at the bar. Then I know you won't get it back until you're sober—otherwise, they won't even let you in.'

Shulte swore again, but Dan Rawley was unimpressed. He awaited, staring the man down, and after a moment Cap Shulte swung his heavy shoulders and went clomping away, taking his grievance and his defeat with him. Dan waited until the sound of his boots on rattling planks had faded, before he let the tension run out of him. He lowered the gun.

The brief moment of excitement had died when there was no repetition of that single gunshot. Such incidents were common enough on the streets of Bellport, and it took something more to create a real disturbance. Dan turned as George Byam stepped up onto the walk beside him and laid a hand in friendly fashion upon his shoulder. 'Good God!' he exclaimed. 'For a minute I didn't know what I'd walked into!'

'Just lucky for me you did,' Dan said, trying to make light of it.

Byam was a freighter, one of the important men of Bellport. He had made a success in the old Santa Fe trade. Now, from greenup till first snow, scarcely a week failed to see at least one of his bull trains leave for the new Denver markets. There could hardly be a greater contrast with the half dozen or fewer that a man like Nate Archer managed to put on the road during a season.

'That Shulte!' he said, in heavy disgust. 'I guess I knew you'd had some trouble with him.

Only glad I'm not the one he's carrying a grudge against!'

'He'll get over it. Let me buy you a drink, George. Looks to me I owe you one.'

'Sounds good.'

They walked into the Bellport House. The bar, here, was the best equipped in town and carried the best stock of whisky. It attracted the better quality of trade and there were no bar girls, no gambling and no raffish entertainment, such as was provided to pull the bull-whackers and riverboat crews into the dives along Water Street. The back bar was ornately carved cherrywood, the chandeliers sparkled with crystal, the walls had red velvet paneling. It was more like a rich man's club than a saloon.

Dan Rawley turned over the captured gun to the bartender on duty, got his promise to see about returning the weapon if Cap Shulte ever showed up with a claim to it, and ordered drinks for himself and Byam. He found that his lethargy of half an hour ago had vanished, for the moment, though he knew it would hit him again when his nerves had had a chance to settle.

George Byam lifted his mustache with thumb and forefinger as he tossed off his drink, and then wiped the back of his hand across it. He was a man in his fifties and prospering, with a thickening middle and well-cut clothing and bench-made boots. Eyeing

46

Dan Rawley, he set the thimble-sized glass down and said, 'I heard something more about you. I heard you went and split the blanket with Nate Archer. Congratulations!'

Dan, taking his time with his own drink, looked at the other in surprise and some chagrin. 'Just where did you pick *that* up?'

'Why, it's all over town. Reckon you didn't know, but some of us have had a bet as to just how long you were going to put up with a man like him.'

Dan frowned. 'I can't imagine what interest it would be to anyone. Besides, Nate and I had different ways at looking at some matters, but our business arrangements were good enough.'

'Sure—sure,' Byam said, and changed the subject. He had a hundred questions to ask about the crossing, about the outlook for business at the mines; about Franklin Owen's new associates and their interests in California Gulch and their plans for the spring—all the questions Nate Archer and Wes Boyd hadn't ever been curious enough to raise. Dan Rawley told him what he wanted to know, and knew that every fact was being ticked and stored away in Byam's shrewd, businessman's brain.

The freighter offered to stand a round, but Rawley shook his head. 'One's my limit.'

'If I can't buy you a drink,' Byam said, 'how about offering you a job? I don't know what Archer paid you, but I'll bet it was damned

47

little for a wagon man of your caliber. Name his price and I'll double it.'

Dan slowly finished his drink as he considered the proposition. It was a good one, and it was sincerely made. But he shook his head. 'I'm afraid not George. I can only tell you what I told Nate Archer: I didn't quit him to look for a better job, but because I have to try it on my own. Any man wants to work for himself.'

Byam looked concerned. 'You got capital?'

'Enough to buy a wagon and the mules to haul it, and still have something to dicker on a first load of merchandise if I can get it cheap enough.' He grinned slightly at the other's expression. 'You're thinking the same thing Nate did: A damned, down-at-the-heels shotgun freighter! But, it's no disgrace to start small. Just means I risk less.'

'Nothing but your skin!' the other corrected him darkly, with a shake of the head. 'A man on his own, or maybe even a couple of them—making that trip! I don't have to tell you what can happen: A breakdown, an accident of any kind; a run in with the redskins! Any single one of these, somewhere between Denver and the River, and chances are nobody will never even know what happened to you.'

'It's my skin,' Dan Rawley reminded him, with a smile at the man's grave expression. 'I've learned a few tricks, I guess, about keeping it all in one piece. Anyway, I've decided this is what I want to do with it.'

'Yeah, I guess you have,' George Byam admitted, scowling. 'And knowing what kind of a mule you are, I'm not so big a fool as to think I could talk you out of it! Well, good luck, anyway. I'm going to be more than interested to see how you make out.'

CHAPTER FIVE

The window of the bank president's office, overlooking the principal street crossing, stood open in the lingering Indian summer weather. Through it came the smell of the River and the busy voice of a thriving port town—a ramble of freight wagons through unpaved streets, the yells of teamsters and the occasional bray of a mule or squeal of a horse, the racket of a hurdy-gurdy pounding away in a neighboring saloon. And against this background, Dan Rawley sat beside an unlittered expanse of polished desk top and told his story. Taggart, the banker, heard him out and turned him down, cold.

After all, Daw Rawley owned no collateral except ambition and experience; and while normally his reputation in itself might have been enough to get him a loan, just now the chaotic situation in Kansas Territory—joined to the uncertainties and anxieties of the

49

coming national election—made for scared money. Taggart would personally have liked to oblige him, but he was sure that Dan understood his position.

Dan took it without a change in expression. He thanked the man, rose, shook his hand, and left. Actually, he was more relieved than anything.

Going to the bank was something he had felt obligated to do, if there was an off chance of financial backing. Now that he'd been refused, he knew he had no choice but to follow his original plan, and he wasn't sure but what he preferred it so. He knew one or two other places he might go—George Byam for one might be willing to let him have something, as Vinnie Owen's father would have done had his resources not been tied up in other ways. But Dan didn't care a great deal about starting out in debt. It was too much like trying to make a standing jump out of a hole.

Better, by his figuring, to start small but independent; then, anything you won was yours and no one else's. By the same token, if you lost, you quit with a clean slate—and no debts hanging over you like the sour taste of the morning after.

With this interview behind him, he dropped down a block to Water Street and entered Milligan's where he knew Hobie Drake would be waiting to hear the outcome. Hobie was seated alone at a table with a schooner of beer in front of him. He read Dan's shake of head, as the latter pulled out a chair.

'Nothing doing, huh? The bastard! Well, I guess we ain't really surprised.' The big fellow sounded cheerful. He dug into a pocket, pulled out a handful of coins and bills and dropped them on the table. Stirring them with a finger, he singled out two gold eagles and pushed them toward his friend. 'Forty bucks left, out of what Archer paid me. Do you any good?'

Dan smiled and shook his head. 'Put it away, friend. If lack of forty dollars can close me out, I might as well go back to working for Archer! Besides, who knows how long you may have to run on that, if you're still set on going in with me?'

Hobie grinned and shoved the money back in his pocket, leaving out a dime for another beer. 'It can last me a damn long time,' he said confidently. 'Especially if I can find me a poker game or two, dealing the right kind of cards. My mama told me never to touch a poker deck, but at that it sounds as safe a gamble as setting up in the freight business!

'And speaking of poker,' he added, his expression changing as his glance moved past Dan Rawley, 'the gent at the bar is the one I was telling you about. The one just lifting his drink . . .'

With a casual movement, Dan hitched about in his chair for a look. He considered the unhealthy appearance of the man—the

51

long, narrow-shouldered shape of him, the bad complexion, the discolored pouches beneath the eyes. 'Know him?' Hobie Drake asked, and when Dan shook his head: 'I done a little asking around. His name's Merrick, and he's been in town a couple of weeks—off the riverboats, would be my guess. He runs a fair-sized game, so he must have a roll or else someone is staking him. Either case, he's a tinhorn—not the company I'd pick, if I had Wes Boyd's responsibilities.'

Dan Rawley considered this as the man at the bar threw off his drink, the red stone on his right hand flashing when he set the empty glass down. The gambler put a coin on the bar, adjusted the set of his wide-brimmed planter's hat and walked out of Milligan's with a slight hint of a swagger. Dan frowned, shook his head. 'It's Wes Boyd's problem. Do you know if they've been playing regular, or was last might maybe the first time?'

'That, nobody's been able to tell me.'

'Well, it's nothing we can interfere in. But I think you'd better be careful, the talking you do. You could start a rumor that way, that would make trouble for Boyd and not help the Owens any.'

Hobie nodded, 'I see what you mean. All right—I'll lay off. Let's talk about our own business . . .'

The big man was in his element when it came to draft teams and rolling stock. 'Your mules will run you something like a hundred apiece, and maybe a couple hundred for the rig. Even if I can talk fast enough to get them to throw in the harness, that looks like six or seven hundred. And I'm afraid they'll want cash.'

'Being pretty damned close to all the cash we've got. Which just means I've got to work some deals to get cargo on credit.'

'You better talk fast, then!' Hobie said. 'I'm glad that isn't my department! Still I should be able to dicker that seven hundred down a little for you. After all, it ain't the time of year when livestock is what you'd call, in demand. I might get us a bargain, from somebody who ain't all that anxious to put out a whole winter's feed bill. As for the wagon: Nothing says we need one right out of the Kansas City yards. Fellow that knows what he's doing can find one that's sort of beat up, and put her in shape himself if her main points are solid.'

'Well, we'll see.' Hobie finished off his second beer, mopped his mouth on a wrist. 'The day's not getting any younger. And time is of the essence. Reckon I better start circulating.'

He scraped back his chair, but he paused as Dan Rawley spoke. 'There's one thing more,' the latter told him. 'I haven't said this before, but I'm saying it now: Since the Lord only knows how soon there's likely to be any profits, or any wages paid around here, it's

53

going to be hard to say who's working for who. Seems to me whatever comes of this venture, we're both in it with all we've got, and should share the same—fifty-fifty, win or lose. How do you like that idea?'

The big fellow stared at him across the empty beer mugs. Slowly his face split in a grin. 'I like it fine!' he grunted. 'Though it's a hell of a lot more than I figured on! Rawley and Drake: step to the bar and I'll drink to that—partner!'

They had their drink and as they parted, their hands met in a gesture that was more binding than any legal document could have been.

From that moment, it seemed there would never be enough time again.

For a shotgun freighter, working as he did on little capital, the difference between success and failure lay in small details and a narrow margin of profit. Dan Rawley did have certain things in his favor: He had just come from the mines, he knew the market there and what was in short supply, and made his rigorous selection of cargo accordingly. He scoured for bargains, following any rumor of a merchant who had laid in an overstock last spring in hopes of catching the flux of gold hunters streaming West, and now wanted to unload. Where it was possible, he gave a deposit, or even his signature; but he didn't hesitate to dip into his slender resources when, for example, he was offered for cash a stack of new tin buckets at a quarter apiece, which he knew would fetch him a dollar or better at Denver City. But each item had to be calculated carefully for its value to the pound, and he could not afford many errors of judgment.

Daily he checked with Hobie Drake. His partner already had an eye on some possibilities in the way of wagons and mules, but he was playing the cards close to his vest, stalling and angling for the right break in price. Dan respected his methods and didn't push him to a decision, though each day spent in this way moved them one day nearer winter—even as the storm clouds of future conflict seemed to settle deeper over the nation with every dispatch that reached them from the East.

A needling rain set in overnight, breaking at last the pleasantness of Indian summer, stripping the last leaves from the cottonwood branches, covering Water Street with a greasy film of mud in which wagon teams struggled and slid to their knees. From the window of his room, where he stood shaving in the bleak light of a clouded morning, Dan Rawley could see a loaded wagon that had skewed sideways and overturned on its way up from the river landing. He was wondering how long he could hope for the empty miles of the trail westward to stay open, when the knock came at the door. He answered it, and frowned in disbelief on confronting Nate Archer.

It was the first time the two had met face to face since the evening he quit his job. And never before had Archer bothered to hunt him down here in his own living quarters. Dan looked at the fleshy face, with its frame of side whiskers. He said without friendliness, 'You wanted to see me?'

Archer nodded shortly and then, as Dan continued to block the doorway, he asked irritably, 'Do I have to be kept standing here in the hall? I've got to talk to you.'

'All right.' Dan stood aside for him. Archer pulled off his plug hat, baring the gleaming dome of his bald head. He stood fiddling with the hat's brim, in a manner that told Dan he was a long way from being at his ease. Dan closed the door, walked around him to the washstand where he splashed his face, took a towel and wiped away what was left of the lather. He was reaching for his shirt as he turned again to his visitor. He said, 'You're early enough.'

'Wanted to be sure I'd find you in. This is pretty important.'

'Well?'

Nate Archer drew a breath. He said gruffly, 'I know we had a little disagreement, the other day, but a man can't afford to be small. I've decided I'm willing to forget about it.'

'Oh, you have?' Dan Rawley would have found this amusing if it were less astounding.

He kept his voice noncommittal, curious to see what the man thought he was talking about.

'I'm willing to forget that you were ready to walk out on me, practically without a word. Now that you've had some time to think things over, I hope you see just how foolish a mistake it was throwing away something as good as you had with me.'

'You'd like to forgive me and let me come back to work, is that it?' Dan interpreted, with a dry sarcasm that was likely lost on the other man. He added flatly, 'Let's hear the rest of it. There has to be more to it than this to drag you here on a rainy morning. What's come up?'

Archer had the grace to color slightly. 'I don't know what call you have, to be suspicious of everything I say! But, as a matter of fact, something *has* come up.' From an inside pocket he drew out a sheaf of papers. 'I received this yesterday from Denver—from Work & Mantley. They have a big consignment of goods arriving on the *River Queen*—probably come up tomorrow. It should make about six wagons, I estimate. And it's got to go forward at once, if I hope to keep their business.

'Look here, Rawley!' The fake pomposity crumbled. Suddenly there were beads of perspiration shining on Nate Archer's bald dome, and his voice held, for once, a trace of honest humility. 'I need help. I'm swallowing my pride, coming here to ask if you'll reconsider. I don't ask out of friendship—you never did like me and I won't pretend it isn't mutual. But I'll pay a good bonus if you'll take these wagons out. This one more time— strictly a business proposition. What do you say?'

And he stood twisting the brim of the plug hat between his soft hands, trying to hide the nervous anxiety that looked out at Rawley from his nearsighted, blinking eyes.

For a moment Dan Rawley actually wavered. It was never pleasant, refusing someone that needed help, and he didn't doubt that this was a very serious thing for Nate Archer. The Work & Mantley account was a big part of his business, and he could hardly afford to lose it. But then the memory of a hundred petty grievances, of chiseling and cheating and shabby treatment at the hands of his employer, rose to stay him. He saw the half-fawning craftiness in the watching eyes, and somehow there was no difficulty in shaking his head.

'Sorry,' he said shortly. 'You've come too late. My plans are set and I've already invested my capital. If I don't get started now it will set me back at least a season.'

'So you're turning me down?' An indrawn breath whistled through the man's suddenly clenched teeth. 'That's all the gratitude—?'

'Let's not go through that again,' Dan

Rawley cut in. 'I don't owe you anything—but I do have an obligation to myself, and to Hobie Drake. You look around, surely you can find someone to take those wagons out for you. You might even think about trying it yourself—you could learn a few things.'

Nate Archer had turned positively ugly. He rammed the hat down on his skull, hard, and glared up at the other from beneath the brim of it. 'I came to you for help—not advice!' At the door, he turned back with his hand already on the knob. 'I ain't gonna forget this, Rawley. Someday you just might wish you hadn't turned your back on me!'

'If that's the way you feel about it,' Dan said shortly, 'I'm sorry. But it's silly to make threats.'

Archer swore at him, and wrenched the door open. It slammed behind him, leaving Dan Rawley frowning at the spot where he had stood.

*   *   *

On an afternoon of shifting cloud shadow and gusty, wet wind, Vinnie Owen and her cousin Wes turned in from the street to enter a gloomy barn by a smaller door cut into the main double leaves that were closed against the weather. Inside was dimness, and the sounds of labor; smells of heated iron and pitch made the girl's nose wrinkle as she lifted the hem of her full skirt, picking a gingerly way among the scraps of machinery and debris that cluttered the uneven floor. The very touch of her cousin's hand at her elbow seemed to speak of his distaste for such surroundings. They were here only because she had insisted.

At the rear of the room, lighted by a single oil lantern hanging from a post, a wagon box stood on blocks, its running gear removed. Hobie Drake and a helper were working at a forge, doing something to the end of a wooden axle while a half-grown boy seated on an empty crate watched as though fascinated. Acrid smoke drifted under the dark ceiling, making Vinnie want to sneeze.

Hobie Drake, turning to pick up a sledge, saw the visitors and greeted them with surprise. 'Careful!' he warned the girl. 'Wouldn't take a minute to ruin that pretty dress.'

'I won't,' she promised. She nodded politely to his assistant, and looked at the little boy. 'This surely doesn't belong to you, Hobie?'

'Him? Oh, no ma'am. That's Bud Crocker—Meg Crocker's youngun. Say hello to the lady, Bud.'

The boy got off his box to do it, and Vinnie smiled as she returned his greeting. She knew something of the boy's mother as an unfortunate and courageous woman. She asked him, 'You intend to work with these big wagons when you grow up?'

60

The youngster merely squirmed a little and grinned, embarrassed beyond answering. 'By the time he's big enough,' Hobie Drake said, 'I reckon us wagon people will long since be out of date. I got a notion there'll be steel rails across the continent, before that.'

Wes Boyd gave a snort. 'I'll believe that when I see it!'

'Keep your eyes open, then,' Hobie said, not bothering to conceal his dislike of the man. 'Little Steve Douglas would have had his railroad bill through Congress a dozen times, if it weren't for them damn—pardon me, Miss Vinnie!—them darned Southern obstructionists!'

Boyd shrugged as though the matter held no interest for him whatever. A door at the rear of the barn opened, then, and Dan Rawley came in.

He set down a pail he was carrying and came to greet his visitors, delighted to see Vinnie, and formally polite to her cousin. To the girl's questions he explained that they were going over every inch of the wagon, repairing everything that showed need of it.

Hobie was just now fashioning a new skein for the front axle end, to fit into the thimble of the wheel. Dan himself had still to finish caulking the cracks with hot pitch, after which a lining with Osnaburg sheeting would make the wagon as tight and waterproof as a boat, against the risk to the cargo in river crossings.

Finally, new iron tires must be shaped and fitted to the big, *bois-d'arc* wheels, and all the wagon's bolt ends securely riveted.

Wes Boyd said, with a hint of amused condescension, 'One wagonload? Is this how you're going to make your fortunes?'

Dan only smiled, not rising to the bait. 'Hardly!' he said. 'This is how we make a start—we hope! Actually, we don't even have a full load, the first trip, because at this time of year we have to carry feed. I've already arranged terms to drop it off and store it at road ranches and stage stations along the route. It's the second trip, next month, when we make a profit.'

'Or lose everything in the drifts, somewhere between here and Denver City,' Wes Boyd suggested.

'Oh, no!' Vinnie cried, reproachfully. 'Nothing of the sort!'

Dan admitted, 'It could happen. But we're betting otherwise. We're betting we clear enough that we can start out next season with a couple of additional outfits, and maybe begin picking up some of the consignment business. Then we'll be on our way.'

Vinnie's cousin gave a shrug, as though he found the whole idea tiresome and a bore. Paying him no heed, she asked, 'Where have you got your mules?'

'In the corral out back,' Dan said. 'I was just giving them some feed. Want a look at them?'

He took the girl's arm and guided her through a door at the rear of the barn. As it closed behind them, Hobie Drake, who had been secretly studying Wes Boyd, asked abruptly: 'How about you, Mister Boyd? You a betting man?'

The other's head whipped about, a suspicious glance pinning the yellow-haired man. His voice held sharp surprise as he demanded, 'Why ask that?'

Hobie was innocently examining the heating of the metal in the forge. 'Oh, I dunno. You don't seem to think much of this proposition of ours. I thought you might be in a mood for putting up a little cash. *Mine* says we'll not only make it up Denver, but we'll be back without a mishap and—I wouldn't wonder—even clear a profit.'

Boyd scowled. 'And, suppose you're wrong?' he pointed out. 'Suppose I win: When you're bleaching out your bones somewhere between here and the mountains—how do I collect?'

'You got a point!' Hobie Drake admitted. He thoughtfully rubbed the ball of a thumb across his soot-streaked jaw. 'Looks like what we need is someone to hold the stakes, somebody we can trust . . .' A bright inspiration appeared to strike him. 'I know just the fellow! Mike Milligan. You ever been in Milligan's, by any chance?'

Now Boyd was scowling, as though almost certain of a trap hidden in the guileless question. He stared at Hobie and then, with another shrug, moved as if to turn away. The intention of dismissing the entire matter was, at that moment, written clear on his face.

'Still,' Hobie said casually, 'if you ain't sure enough to want to lay your money on the line, I reckon that should make me feel a sight more confident.'

That decided Wes Boyd. He said abruptly, 'How much you want to bet? A hundred?'

Hobie blinked. 'Kind of steep, for me!' he started to object; then abruptly changed his mind. 'But, what the hell—this is too good a thing to pass up. I can borrow the difference from Milligan. You meet me at his place this evening. We'll set up the bet, and have a drink on it.'

Wes Boyd had a look of not knowing exactly how he had become involved in this, but he nodded curtly. 'I'll be there. Seven o'clock. But don't expect me to wait around for you.'

'You won't have to,' Hobie assured him. 'Not a chance.'

At the pen in back of the barn, Dan and Vinnie were regarding the four mules which, just now, were working on the grain he had dumped into their troughs. Vinnie exclaimed admiringly, 'They look so *big* when you see them close like this. Much bigger than horses.'

'These are big fellows, all right,' Dan agreed. 'I'd be careful,' he added, as the girl stepped nearer and placed a hand on one of the bars.

One big mule had left the trough and was approaching the fence with mincing steps, his neck stretched out and the tall ears semaphoring. Suddenly the ears lay flat; huge yellow teeth snapped as the animal lunged without warning, and Vinnie squealed and backed off, snatching her hand away. Dan caught her shoulders, steadying her. Hearing her shaky laugher, he exclaimed, 'You aren't hurt?' He was sure his face was as white as her own.

'No,' she gasped. 'But he—he tried to take my hand off! Dan, I think that animal is *wild!*'

'He is, a little,' Dan admitted, making no move to release her, since she didn't seem in a hurry to free herself. 'A couple of them, in fact. Hobie was able to get a good bargain, because they're not too well broke in yet.'

She stared at him. 'But—how can you use anything like that? You'll both be killed!'

He grinned and shook his head. 'Hobie knows what he's doing. Our other pair is a trained, matched team. Look, and you can see the harness marks on them. So don't worry— they'll take no nonsense off these green wheelers. If they act up, the leaders will kick the whey out of them. Hundred miles or so should teach them their manners.'

'Oh, Dan . . .' Her eyes, and the shake of her head, were gravely concerned. She asked, 'When—when do you leave?'

'If we can finish working on the wagon tonight and get loaded, we pull out early in the morning.'

'And will I see you first?'

He said soberly, 'Afraid I can't promise that. We hope to get an early start.' A smile broke across his dark face. 'But you'll see me sure, after I get back!'

She tried to answer his smile, and make her answer as light and full of confidence. 'Of course, Dan. And—I'll be praying for good weather. All the way, and back again.'

CHAPTER SIX

A prairie chicken burst out of cover some dozen paces in front of Dan Rawley's horse, and like a well-trained plains animal, the bay froze, standing rock-steady under him as he brought up the Sharps. The report was swallowed up in the flat immensity of the land, and the bird tumbled and plummeted in a shower of feathers. Without being told, the bay walked forward then, and Dan swung down to retrieve his kill.

It was a fat specimen and, together with the others in his saddlebags, would add flavor to rations that after a week were already growing monotonous. He stowed it away and reloaded the gun. But then he had a look at the angle of the sun and, deciding he had bagged enough for the day's needs, he turned and pointed east again toward the trail.

A desolate and empty world, out here. The cloud ceiling hung in dirty rolling billows, like the sagging canvas of a tent pressing low above the brown and rolling plains. South of the Platte, still a day from Fort Kearney, the land was arid and treeless—no wood at all, and no water except where recent rains had filled up the sloughs to some extent. Game was sparse after a season of especially heavy travel. Dan had had to range considerably west and north in his search for fresh meat this afternoon. Once he had seen a band of pronghorns but too far distant to go after them, and there had been the spoor of a small herd of buffalo— probably an outrider of one of those massive waves of the ungainly beasts that sometimes filled the earth to the horizon and made the ground tremble with their passage.

Human life was even scarcer. In season, the trail was virtually solid with the wagons of freight outfits and goldstrike boomers, but now the tide was down to a trickle. In a day's ride, one saw perhaps a couple of late-returning bull trains, their wagons empty and double-hitched for the final haul to the Missouri. Each time, as was the custom of the trail, Dan Rawley sought out the wagon master for an exchange on the state of things ahead: A man venturing into this emptiness could often owe his life to such gleanings of information.

Now he sent his bay horse up a long, lifting roll of land and, as this broke away, the trail itself lay below him. He pulled up, thumbed the hat back from his head and leaned both wrists on the saddle horn while he studied it as though it were a familiar face.

It stretched generally northward, toward the sand hills of the Platte River Valley that lay somewhere beyond the horizon—there were other, more direct ways to the Denver diggings, along the Republican and Smoky Hill routes that lay west of the Kansas ports; but those were treacherous and men had learned not to trust them. The Overland, though no one had deliberately laid it out, was a real and definite thoroughfare just the same: A road some hundred yards or more in width, beaten smooth by countless hoofs and wagon wheels, scoured clean by steady winds; while at the end of a busy season like this one, a wide margin of grass on either side might be eaten back and cropped clean.

Peering ahead, Dan discovered a thing that held him a moment, frowning in puzzlement. He had seen it there an hour ago and still it hadn't moved. Unmistakably, it was a string of a half dozen wagons. They hadn't been drawn off the trail, or put into corral. They were stretched out in line of march, their canvas gilded faintly now where the rays of the dropping sun, finding an opening in the clouds banked along the horizon, streaked through and touched them as it lighted up the underbellies of the lumpy cloud ceiling.

Those motionless wagons were an unnatural, and therefore troubling sight; they had Dan Rawley frowning as he turned back and rode down off the hill, heading south to look for Hobie Drake who should soon be overtaking him. Even though it was not strictly any of his business, he knew all at once he would not rest well until he had investigated. In this country, you didn't just ignore another man's distress.

Hobie was making camp when Dan Rawley rode in on him—they carried a good supply of water on the wagon, but Drake had found a collection in a slough and had chosen it as a likely place to pull off the road and unhitch the mules, so they could have a roll and drink as much as they wanted. The day was ending in a murky sunset, like a bruise.

While Hobie finished working with his teams—putting them on picket and breaking out a quart of grain apiece for them—Dan dismounted, stowed the Sharps away under the wagon's seat, and began assembling a fire. Their camp seemed small and vulnerable, engulfed by the immensity of the plains and by a silence that was complete except for what sounds they made themselves: The crackle of the flames, the mules working at their dinners, an occasional word from one of the men. Beyond the circle of the fireglow, reflected on the canvas sheeting of the big wagon, a still, cold dusk began to settle.

Dan took from his saddlebag the birds he'd shot. He told his partner, 'Look. Before I can eat, I figure I got another ride to make. I might as well do it while there's still some light.' As he told of those apparently stranded wagons, the fireglow revealed Hobie Drake's scowl.

'Sounds damned peculiar, all right. Still, we're less than a day from Kearney. If they need help they'll likely have sent someone ahead.'

'That may be. But again, maybe they couldn't.'

'What are you thinking? We're too close to the fort, and too far east for real Indian trouble.'

Dan nodded. 'True enough. But it seems only right to check.'

His partner shrugged. 'Suit yourself. I'll hold off dinner. But—be careful you don't walk into anything. I can remember seeing cholera go through a bunch of wagons and leave it gutted—nothing but the dead and dying.'

'I'd thought of that myself,' Dan Rawley said. 'I don't figure to take any chances.'

He checked his cinch, stepped into the saddle and turned the bay north along the trail again. Night was settling fast, with a single star showing behind a gap in the cloud ceiling, where day was dying over to the west. A cold wind had risen; it swept the plains, seeming to blow through that gap and promising clear weather. A coyote's yapping cry sang across the emptiness.

The light was fading fast but there was still a gray glimmering of dusk—enough that as he came nearer he could make out the ghostly glimmer of the wagon sheeting, motionless against gathering night. At a little distance he pulled in. There was no sign of a light, no glow of a fire; and no sound, except occasionally something that struck his trained ear as the familiar sounds of oxen stirring in the traces.

That made it all the stranger. Those wagons were standing with teams still yoked and hitched. But, where were the men?

When he rode forward again, he was somehow strangely reluctant about going directly in toward the wagons. He pulled wide instead, intending first to ride a wary circle and try to get some clearer idea of what was wrong. He went at a walk, circling out of the hard-beaten surface of the trail and into stubble that had been grazed down nearly to the roots. And being so intent on hunting for any sign of movement among the wagons, he had no warning of danger until the merest whisper of movement suddenly pulled his head around.

The upward end of a shallow draw, choked with brush, opened a few yards to his right.

71

Out of this, barely disturbing the shadowy growth that had given it cover, a shape was hurtling straight at him. Dan Rawley groped for the cap-and-ball pistol in his belt holster but even as it cleared the holster he was struck. Clawing fingers clutched at him, a knifeblade glinted; the bay shied under him and Dan, concerned with avoiding the keen point of the blade, was unable to keep his saddle. It moved from under him and he and his silent attacker were going down together.

He lost his gun, felt greasy buckskin under his frantically groping fingers, smelled the rancid, stomach-turning odor that meant Indian. There was a gusting of breath expelled from that other pair of lungs as the two men hit the ground solidly in a tangle. Stiff, coarse hair swept across Dan's face. And then they were rolling in a silent, life-and-death grapple for possession of the knife.

He had never fought so desperately. Hampered by the blackness he struck blindly, blows that couldn't seem to find a target. At the same time, he was striving frantically to locate the hand which held the weapon, as a slime of sweat burst from every pore. Suddenly it was as though a white-hot wire had been drawn across his ribs. He gasped with the shock of the blade, and next moment his hand clamped down upon an arm that seemed all rawhide and iron-hard tendon.

The other man was smaller, tighter of

frame, but with the tough, lithe agility of an animal. Grappling, they rolled over chill, damp mud, and after that were into the brush where the attacker had lain concealed. This halted them, with Dan Rawley on the bottom. A hand raked across his eyes and face, clawing at his throat. Somehow, he retained his grip on the knife-arm, and the ground against his back gave him purchase. With strength he didn't know he had, Dan gave a wrenching heave of his whole body. The weight on top of him was suddenly dislodged, and hurled straight over his head.

He lost his hold. As the Indian crashed into spiny brush, Dan rolled and scrambled, panting, to his knees. His right hand, touching the ground for balance, came in contact with a sizable rock. He clamped on it, seeking a weapon. It was embedded in the dirt and for a moment resisted his clawing fingers. Then he got a better grip and tore it up out of the ground, damp and gritty.

Already free of the brush and on his feet again, the Indian came at him—a dimly-glimpsed shape against grainy darkness, almost silent in his hurtling rush. Dan, still on his knees, brought his arm back and around in a blind arc. He felt the rock in his fist land solidly against the side of the man's head; the Indian was flung in a sprawl, face down. He was already struggling to rise as Dan Rawley, kneeling over him, struck him a second time, and then a third, on the back of his skull.

He felt bone give way. Suddenly the man was still, and Dan flung the rock far from him and shaking in every limb, fought the nausea that churned into his throat.

Only an Indian—but he had been a man, the first Dan Rawley had killed. And the killing had been peculiarly horrible.

Where there had been one, however, there could be more; it was this thought that helped to settle him and sent him hunting for his gun. He found where it had fallen from his holster, and he picked it up and shook dirt from the muzzle, checking the loads by touch to make sure the caps hadn't been dislodged from the nipples. As he stood holding the gun and studying the stillness, his bay horse came walking up out of the dusk and nuzzled his arm. He patted the animal's neck idly.

Again he studied that strange line of motionless wagons, much closer now, while he shoved a hand in under his jacket and shirt to test the damage the knife had done. It was painful, as any cut is, but it had merely raked his ribs and appeared to have quit bleeding quickly. Still, it was enough to start his sweating again, realizing just how close a thing that had been. His hand was trembling slightly when he rebuttoned the shirt, leaving the cut to be tended to later.

Something was going on, over there on the far side of the wagons. He could hear someone

74

moving about—a bang of metal, a mutter of voices. Now, as he watched, a glow of fire began to show, silhouetting a set of wheel spokes and underrigging. It strengthened, as fuel was thrown on. A man's legs moved jerkily across it.

Dan Rawley shoved revolver into holster. Taking the reins, he led his horse over to the Indian he had killed, and although the bay snorted protest at the smell of blood, he made it stand. The body was not heavy and he was able to lift it and sling it, belly down, across the saddle. He steadied it there, and started toward the wagons.

Nearing, he could see the patient oxen standing or lying under the yokes. A solitary white horse with a saddle on its back was tied to a wagon tailgate where it stood out almost like a beacon. It stomped uneasily as Dan led his horse with its grisly burden between a couple of the big freight rigs, and into the light of the fire.

The flames were burning well, trailing fountains of sparks and placing their warm glow on stretched canvas. It was now, too, that they showed him the letters stenciled on the nearest wagonbox: NATHAN ARCHER. And, with that, a lot of things suddenly seemed clearer.

At first Dan could see only one man, who stood looking stupidly at the fire and rubbing his head with both hands. When he happened

75

to look up and saw what was moving out of the shadows he went motionless—hair awry, both arms lifted. Then slowly, as though he remembered he had them, he dropped his hands to his sides. His name was Tucker, and he had worked under Dan Rawley on other trains.

'What's goin' on here, Tuck?' Dan asked him. 'What's wrong with this outfit?'

Tucker ran his tongue around inside his mouth, across his teeth. When he spoke he sounded as though the tongue had fur on it. 'A little trouble. Nothing important. Wagon smashed a wheel.'

He made a vague, backwards gesture. Peering beyond him, Dan saw the situation. One of the rigs was indeed disabled. It leaned crazily on three wheels and an axle end. The big ironshod wheel lay in the dirt amid a scatter of tools, a couple of its spokes shattered beyond repair.

Dan Rawley scowled. 'When did that happen?'

The man lifted a shoulder. 'Sometime this morning, I guess. We been working on it.'

'This morning!' Walking over for a closer look at the damage, Dan saw that crates and boxes had been unloaded from the wagon bed and stacked about, lightening it to facilitate repairs. And then he stopped short, staring at a barrel whose lid had been knocked loose and laid aside. The reek of the contents told him all he needed to know.

He looked again at Tucker. 'So *that's* how it is! When you stopped for an accident, you found there was a barrel of whisky aboard and the damn thing turned into a party!' Anger and scorn sharpened his voice. 'What finally sobered you enough to get you on your feet, and a fire built? Did you realize you were freezing to death?'

Tucker was scowling, a look of sodden belligerence on his face, his head swinging a little from side to side. 'Go to hell, Rawley! You ain't telling nobody what to do. You ain't bossing this outfit!'

'Is anybody?' he retorted, disgustedly. He looked around. Other men were edging up out of the shadow, now, into the ring of light and warmth from the fire. They had the look of men who had drunk too much and too fast. One big Swede, who looked positively green, had been sick on himself and his clothing reeked with the foulness of it. Dan Rawley demanded, 'Somebody speak up! Who's responsible? Who's supposed to be in charge of this outfit?'

A familiar shape pushed forward, shouldering the sick and unsteady figures of the half dozen teamsters out of the way. Cap Shulte stood swaying, his eyes glinting wickedly in the fireglow. 'You're looking at him, Rawley.'

Dan could only stare, for a moment. 'You,

Shulte? *You've* been promoted to wagon boss?' He had already guessed this was the Work & Mantley train he might have been taking west for Nate Archer. Until this moment, occupied as he'd been with his own affairs, he hadn't given the matter another thought after turning down Nate's offer that morning at the rooming house. He had merely taken for granted the shipment must have gone out, some days past. Considering the relative rate of travel of the ponderous ox teams and his faster moving mules, it was inevitable Dan should expect to overtake it. But, it had never once occurred to him he would find Shulte in charge of the job he had refused. He almost felt a twinge of guilt.

Yet he really couldn't hold himself to blame for the mess he saw here. He shook his head as he said sourly, 'I just can't believe Nate couldn't have found better. Why, in any of those saloons on Water Street he ought to have turned up a dozen who'd do this well. He sure as the very devil couldn't have picked worse!'

'Damn you!' Cap Shulte loosed a bellow of pure rage and launched himself at his enemy. Befuddled though he might be by the whisky he'd consumed, the brute centers of his consciousness would still be functioning, making him a dangerous foe if he could once get those tremendous hands on him. This was in Dan Rawley's mind as he faded back, aware

78

of the stupefied and staring men around them—knowing, this time, no George Byam would step in to pick his enemy off him.

He discovered he had one of the big wagons at his back and, trying to avoid that trap, moved hastily aside and so directly into the path of a reaching fist. It struck him in the chest with force enough to crush the wind from his lungs, and drove him staggering back against the iron edge of a wheel that was as tall as he was. The wrenching impact stretched that raw knife-cut, started the warm blood flowing over his ribs. Dan braced himself, waiting as Shulte came lumbering in to close and finish him.

The big man was wide open, too eager to get his hands on his enemy, too contemptuous to bother about protecting himself from a blow. Even so, Dan doubted that he could hurt the brute with an ordinary punch. He lifted both fists together, and with the full weight of shoulders and forearms swung a clubbing smash at the point where the thick neck joined the body. It landed solidly. An arm went numb as it struck the solid bone of the shoulder, but the blow brought Shulte's head down and drove a grunt of pain from him. He faltered and then came on again, trying now to wrap his arms around his opponent.

Dan set his back against the wheel and lifted a knee, hard, against the lowered head. It didn't land squarely, but it grazed a cheek and it broke the charge, sending Shulte back a pace. Firelight shone wetly on blood that had sprung out upon the beard-stubbled cheek. Cap Shulte roared his fury, shaking his head.

Suddenly Dan remembered he had a gun in his holster. With no compunction at all, he grabbed for it as Cap came on once more, and lifting it from leather, struck with the barrel at the Dutchman's bullet head—knowing he had to end this, aware that he was already near exhaustion from his battle to the death with the Indian.

Cap Shulte was stopped, on his feet but flung clear around by the impact. Still carried by the impetus of his rush, he went weaving blindly, in a drunken run, with knees lifted high and staggering at every step until he collided full tilt against the opened whisky barrel, and took it over with him. Man and barrel went down together, the rest of the whisky pouring out in a flood. Breathing hard, Dan Rawley turned the muzzle of his gun on the half dozen others.

There seemed to be no fight in any of them. They looked stupidly at Cap Shulte, sprawled in a sodden heap, and then lifted their stares at Dan. He shook his head, in anger and contempt.

'I got something I want to show this crowd.'

Their eyes following him dumbly, he holstered his gun and walked over to lead his bay horse out of the shadows, into the firelight where they could see, for the first time, what was draped across the saddle. He grabbed a handful of buckskin clothing and dumped the dead Indian onto his back on the ground. Suppressing a shudder as he got his own first real look at the grisly thing, he saw now it was the body of a Cheyenne, a young buck, his features slack and bloody.

There was a stir and a shocked murmur among the wagon men. Dan Rawley told them, 'I flushed this out of the brush where he was sneaking up on you. There'll be more around. It's not usual to see them this far east, but I ran across sign of buffalo today and likely he's from a hunting party. Probably he took a dare from the others to sneak in alone and grab off that horse I see tied yonder—that's all the bait he would need. The shape you were in, he and his friends could just as easily have slit all your throats for you!'

He let this sink in as he looked around at the sick and sobering faces. He nodded bleakly. 'Now you know!' he said. 'But I'm going to leave him here to remind you.'

Deliberately, Dan turned and swung into the saddle. From there, reins in his hand, he told them, 'If there's any sense left in this bunch, you'll get to work. Unyoke those teams, for God's sake; make a proper camp. Get that wheel changed and the wagon loaded so you can roll, come morning. And if you find any more barrels like that one under Cap Shulte—

forget it!'

They looked thoroughly chastened, ready to obey. But yonder, Shulte sat like a lump, in a broadening circle of spilled whisky; and he lifted a bloody, angry face. 'You ain't giving orders here!'

'Then you'd better start giving them,' Dan said flatly. 'Or, the way things are going, this train will never see Denver. Not that it matters to me,' he added gruffly. 'Except, even Nate Archer deserves better from a wagon boss—even from one like you.'

At that Cap Shulte lumbered to his feet. 'One of these days,' he promised, 'I'm gonna kill you.'

Dan Rawley didn't bother to answer. He reined his horse around and rode it out of the firelight, leaving them irresolutely staring after him with the dead Indian on the ground at their feet.

The thick night swallowed him. He never once looked back.

CHAPTER SEVEN

Stirring in his blankets, Dan Rawley opened his eyes and after a moment hitched up onto an elbow, not at all sure what had roused him. A cold stillness lay over the camp; his breath hung in a faintly visible cloud, and dawn was the barest hint of brightness along the edges of the rolling prairie.

The clouds had scattered and stars dominated the sky, shaking down a faint glimmer of light. Frost sparkled on the ground like jewels.

Nearby, the bay horse moved restlessly and now he knew that this was the sound that had reached him, just below the level of consciousness, to bring him awake. It was a signal that he knew better than to ignore. He draw his boots to him and pulled them on, and then from under his blankets brought out his revolver, its metal chill to the touch. Holding it he eased to a stand beside the silent bulk of the big wagon, and the dead campfire ashes.

No sound or movement, now, except for one of the mules stirring on the picket line and then settling again. Dan moved over and knelt by the wagon, reaching under to lay a hand on Hobie Drake's shoulder. He felt his partner's movement as the latter came quickly awake. 'Easy!' he warned in a whisper. 'The animals are acting up. I think we got company.'

Quickly Hobie joined him beside the wagon, carrying the Sharps. They stood keening the dawn wind, straining for sound. Hobie said, 'They could of smelled coyote.'

'They could,' Dan Rawley admitted. 'But after what nearly happened to me last night we know there's Indians around. Four good mules and the bay would look awfully tempting. And this is just the time of day they'd likely make a play for them.'

Hobie said grimly, 'Let 'em try!'

Moments dragged out. A dawn wind began to freshen, bringing the raw smell of endless prairies and slapping the canvas against the wagon's bows in a way that thwarted their efforts to hear. Dan Rawley stepped clear of the wagon and circled the place where the mules were picketed. He could see them dimly, only one standing, the others lying down. The light was strengthening; as the stars faded, pools of ground water reflected a blank, steel-gray sky.

He pivoted slowly where he stood, running a glance all around the skyline—and suddenly dropped to one knee, revolver resting on thigh. For a moment he thought he'd been mistaken; then a shadow separated itself from the black line of a low hill, took on the crouching shape of a man. The Indian waited, and seeming to sense no danger moved forward at a silent running prowl. Deliberately, Dan Rawley fired.

He shot twice, and saw the black silhouette collapse. He thought he had made a hit but couldn't be sure—the man might only have been dropping into cover. But there was no time to wonder about it, for almost as though his shots had been a signal, the early dawn quite suddenly burst apart.

All at once horses were running, their hoofs

84

pounding prairie hardpan; thin, gobbling cries swelled in savage throats, guns boomed and Hobie Drake's rifle was slamming back as fast as he could fire and load. Dan forgot that one Indian he might or might not have accounted for, as he turned to circle the wagon again, at a run. The half-wild mules were up and milling. And now, as he rounded the tailgate, from still another direction he saw them come—a line of horsemen, seven or eight, sweeping toward them across a swell of prairie. He put his back against the wagonbox and, braced there, drew the best bead he could and added the flat crack of the hand gun to Hobie Drake's rifle.

The raiders seemed almost to run into an invisible wall. Thrown into confusion by the unexpected gunfire, they pulled up in a mill of half-seen shapes, of squealing horses and half-human cries. Dan Rawley poured shot after shot into them, feeling he could hardly miss some kind of target. A rifle answered in a gout of muzzle flame. A flung lance came streaking, to stab the earth not a foot away from Hobie Drake and sway there.

Calmly ignoring it, Hobie aimed and picked one of the riders off the back of his pony, dropped him spinning. That had a magical effect. The uncanny animal cries took on a different sound. The attack hung fire as the remaining half dozen seemed to lose their nerve. Suddenly, with one purpose, they whirled their horses and went pouring back up

85

the slope, brandishing lances and long guns in a last futile gesture of defiance. They were skylighted briefly, against the brightening sky, and dropped from sight. It was all over, as quickly as that.

Dan Rawley lowered his smoking pistol that still had a couple of loads left in it. His breathing was shallow in his throat and the bandaged knife cut across his ribs ached dully. He looked at his partner, who stood with rifle reloaded and ready as he squinted at the empty line of the ridge.

'That ought to be it,' Dan said.

Hobie looked somewhat dubious, but he relaxed his tense pose and lowered the rifle. 'You think so?'

'There was only a handful—probably friends of the one I killed last night. Just a bunch of young bucks, ranging far afield and with no real leader. I doubt they'll be back for more of what we gave them.'

'You're probably right.' But Hobie added, 'Just the same, let's not waste any time. Let's hitch up and get out of here!'

'Suits me,' Dan Rawley said. Sobered, they proceeded to break camp as full daylight came upon the world, and sky and prairie began to take on the colors of bleak autumn.

Toward mid-morning they passed the Archer train, giving it a wide berth. The teamsters who stumbled alongside, cursing their animals and laying about with the ugly bullwhips, looked sick and hungover. After last night it was a wonder, in Dan Rawley's opinion, that Cap Shulte had managed to get them—or himself—on the trail at all.

Riding at the head of the wagons, the big Dutchman sat his saddle like a lump. When he recognized Rawley his head pulled up and for a moment it looked as though he wanted more trouble; but Dan held his bay steady and paid him no attention. Anyone else he would have hailed, with a warning of the dawn attack; but if Cap Shulte didn't know by now to keep on the alert for Indian trouble, there was not much point in reminding him.

Dan Rawley was just as happy when the faster-moving mule team pulled ahead, and Nate Archer's wagons were left behind.

At Fort Kearney, on the great sagging bend of the Platte River, all the raveled ends of the Overland—the separate strands leading in from the many individual Missouri River ports—finally knitted together. At this grubby little post, protecting all westward travel, there was a last chance for major repairs; and so the partners spent the waning hours of an afternoon going over the wagon for weaknesses that might have developed since they left Missouri. Some of the harness showed signs of wear and had to be replaced, and a check must be made on the irons of their stock, all round—they carried no forge and a thrown shoe could mean real trouble.

Next morning, after a final drink at a bar in the raw settlement called Dobytown, a couple of miles west of the fort, Dan and Hobie struck west into the emptiness of the Plains, with no real stopping place between this point and Denver at the mouth of Cherry Creek. By the time they pulled out of Kearney, Cap Shulte and the Archer wagons hadn't yet come into sight. At its best, a bull train would travel at scarcely half the speed of a lone mule wagon. Barring some accident of their own, they were not apt to be encountering Shulte's outfit again, this side of Denver City.

Taking turn about on the wagon and in the saddle, the partners traversed a deserted world. The Platte bottom lay wide and barren, little more than a waste of sand that held, at this time of year, only an occasional stretch of stagnant water; and they had this world almost to themselves. In season, from April till fall, the hard-packed road was a busy one—nearly a continuous stream of wagon traffic, so that a man on horseback could ride it for days on end and never be out of sight of fellow travelers. To one used to seeing it like that, it looked strangely empty now.

Almost the only human life to be encountered was at the stage stations or at the occasional road ranch. Here a few lonely men maintained a kind of existence, made either garrulous or short of speech according to their temperaments, and wary-eyed from the constant vigil against a surprise attack that could come at any time in Indian country. Altogether, in all this slow stretch of miles, Rawley and Drake met no more than three wagon outfits, one of these westward bound and the others returning. A couple of times, too, stage coaches rolled up out of the far emptiness and went boiling past, with a wave and a shout from driver and guard and top-deck passengers.

Once, lying in his blankets beside a dead fire, Dan Rawley heard the rhythmic music of a single galloping horse swell and fade against the black sounding board of the night. He came to his feet to peer into the darkness, but the rider was gone again before he could get so much as a glimpse of the shadowy shape of man or horse. He stood for a long moment, hearing Hobie Drake's uninterrupted snoring and thinking of that lone rider, pounding along these starlit miles that linked the ends of the continent.

You had to respect the raw courage and endurance of the men who carried the pony mail.

Constantly, the wind blew; the days grew shorter, the nights colder. The mules, half-wild at starting, were fairly broken to the harness by now. Hobie Drake's single-load Sharps regularly brought down meat to augment the food they carried with them. Game became more plentiful. Almost every mile showed some movement of wild life—a wedge of geese making their fluting music overhead, a cloud of antelope darkening the distance with their rush, prairie dogs whistling from their holes.

When, almost without warning, a sound like summer thunder swelled below the horizon, Dan Rawley knew instinctively what it meant and abruptly hauled the bay around to spur it toward the wagon. Hobie Drake had halted his team and had the rifle across his lap as the rumble grew and loudened. And then, across a rise, the forerunners of the buffalo herd swept ponderously into view—a solid wall, heads down, hoofs and horns glinting splintered flashings of sunlight, tremendous shoulders working.

They were a wave that would hopelessly engulf the wagon and its team. Racing nearer, Dan Rawley saw Hobie stand now and lift the rifle to his shoulder, afterward slowly lowering it without wasting the shot. It was a futile gesture, for nothing in the world could stop that juggernaut of massive flesh and horn and hoof. Shoulders settling resignedly, Hobie stood and watched it come.

Then Dan was pulling abreast of the wagon, and swinging the bay in a fast turn while he kicked a stirrup free and reached a hand. His voice was almost lost in the deafening roar that shook the ground under them and drove the mules half-crazy in the harness. 'Quick! On behind!' They had no chance of saving the wagon, but a horse might reach safety before the tide struck.

But Hobie was staring past him and shaking his head with an unreadable expression. Dan Rawley turned in the saddle and saw that, for some unexplainable brute reason, the edge of the herd was veering away. It dipped into a swale and topped a farther rise, missing by half a hundred yards the spot where the wagon stood. Knife-sharp hoofs chopped at the sod and a column of yellow dust rose for the wind to flatten and whip away across the backs of the running beasts as they poured past, now, in a seemingly endless tide.

Hobie Drake showed Dan a sickly grin, in a face that was pale behind its mask of blond beard stubble. His lips moved; Dan managed to read the words he couldn't hear: 'I guess that wasn't the time!'

After that, Hobie dropped to his seat, stowed the rifle away and fought the mules under control. Dan Rawley, kicking the bay forward to the near leader, grabbed the headstall. Together the partners got the teams into line and moved them to safety, away from the still too-near thunder of mindless peril.

Dan Rawley could feel his arms shaking in their sockets, and fear in his throat like a lump he couldn't swallow. After a close escape like that one, you couldn't help but wonder how long it took a man to use up his full quota of luck.

Denver had surely grown, even since they pulled out with the last Archer train. So it seemed to Dan Rawley who had watched the place spring up almost from its beginnings as a poverty-stricken, hope-ridden camp on the mud banks where Cherry Creek met the South Platte. He could hardly believe, now, that that had been no more than a year and a half ago. From one visit to the next, Dan felt he scarcely recognized the place.

Even now, with winter already whitening the upward reaches of the mountain wall behind it, Denver City buzzed with growth and with boisterous life. A steady banging of hammers marked the erection of new buildings from milled lumber, rising among the crude pole and canvas shelters of the camp's first beginnings. A swarm of humanity crowded the muddy gashes that served for streets, and all the saloons roared at midday. No man could help but respond to the vitality and crudeness of the place.

The partners looked for Frank Owen and located him, as they would have expected, in his store on F Street. It was a substantial place of business, built of adobe and laid out on generous lines for growth. They found Owen giving orders to a battery of three busy clerks. He greeted Dan with pleasure, shook hands with them both and took time to show them into his bachelor quarters at the rear of the store, where he insisted on pouring a shot of good rye whisky all around.

'It sits well on a man's stomach, a day like this,' he said, and nodded above his drink as a whooping burst of wind pummeled the window, scouring the glass with stinging rain, carrying a hint of winter off the high Rockies. Vinnie Owen's father was a tall, well built man, still youthful except that his black hair was thinning and sprinkled faintly with gray. His shrewdly intelligent, businessman's eyes were a clear gray like his daughter's.

Hobie Drake smacked his lips as he sampled the rye and let it burn the chill out of him. His mind was still full of what they had seen since their arrival and he asked, 'Don't they ever turn this place off?'

'Denver's a twenty-four hour camp,' the other agreed. 'Right about now, as winter begins to close out the high country, the boys come down out of the hills where some of them haven't seen a town since spring. A lot will be leaving, but the rest will hole up with us until the passes open again. And the ones that bring gold dust with them will keep things rocking till then.

'Business is almost as good up in those camps in Gregory Gulch. And my friends and I are betting our rolls that California Gulch will turn out even bigger.' There was a government map on the wall and Frank Owen got up from his chair to point out the location of the gulch, north and west of Denver, at the headwaters of the Arkansas. 'There's good color, every indication that someday it's going to be a real strike. I think it would be well worth your while to have a look at Oro City. Come to think of it, I'm running up there tomorrow for a couple of days. I'll be glad to show you around.'

Hobie started to say that that sounded like a fine thought, but Dan Rawley interrupted with an abrupt shake of the head. 'No time,' he said flatly. 'By tomorrow I've got to have this cargo disposed of and be ready to start back.'

They stared at him. 'Start back!' Owen exclaimed. 'Already? You're crowding yourself hard, boy.'

'The calendar's crowding me.' He put down his empty glass and stood, bone-weary but restless. 'One thing you can do, if you will: Let it out that we're accepting fares East. We can handle half a dozen passengers, and a reasonable amount of luggage. We'll charge one-half the rate they would pay on the Leavenworth stage. Have anyone that's interested get in touch with Drake.' He looked at his partner. 'I'll depend on you to screen the applicants. Cash or gold dust on the line, and we want no one who can possibly hold us back in any way. We pull out at dawn. That all clear?'

Hobie blinked. 'Why sure. Sure, Dan. I'll take care of it.'

'Good,' Dan told the merchant: 'Thanks for the drink. Right now I got a wagonload of stuff to dispose of. I better get at it.'

Frank Owen said, nodding, 'Of course.' He added, 'I'm pretty well stocked, myself. But anything you want me to, I'll be glad to handle for you on consignment.'

'I might have to take you up on that,' Dan Rawley said, and left. For a moment the other two looked at each other in sober silence.

'A good man,' Owen commented, wagging his head. 'Ambitious.'

Hobie Drake scowled into his glass. 'I'm beginning to find that out. Sometimes it worries me a little.'

'Nothing wrong with ambition,' the older man said quickly. 'A man needs a spur. Mine brought me to Kansas, five years ago—and now it's put me here.'

Hobie nodded. 'Guess I always been a shade too easy going. Probably the best thing could happen, that I have someone like Dan Rawley to haul me along.' But there was reluctance in his movements, as he finished off his drink and pushed back the chair. 'Much as I'd admire to, I can't set here taking it easy while my partner works. If we're hauling passengers back in that wagon, I got to rig up something for seats.'

He was starting to turn to the door when a

thought made him pause. 'Something I'd about decided not to mention,' he said, hesitantly. 'And I'm probably talking out of turn. But back there in Bellport—that fellow you got running things . . .'

'My nephew?' Owen frowned. 'What about him?'

'Nothing that's any of my business; but I just ain't sure he keeps the best company. I've seen him a couple of times, hanging out at Milligan's with a gent that has "cardshark" writ all over him. Boyd was playing poker—and losing.' Hobie lifted a shoulder inside his heavy, thrown-open coat, 'I wonder if you knew how he was spending his time.'

Owen frowned, his gray eyes troubled. 'No, I didn't know,' he said. 'I admit I've been a little disappointed in young Boyd. In fact, it would suit me if he could be more like your friend Rawley, but I suppose this country doesn't hold much to interest him.'

'And that sends him to Milligan's . . .' Hobie shrugged. 'Well, no harm in it I guess,' he said, deciding to make light of the thing now that he'd aired his vague suspicions. 'So long's he don't get in too deep. He don't look to me like too hell of a much at poker!'

'He's got good enough sense,' the merchant answered quickly. 'He wouldn't make a fool of himself. And I'm sure he wouldn't let it interfere with managing the business.'

'I'm sure you're right,' Hobie said, and left.

But for long minutes after Hobie was gone, the older man stood motionless, his back to the government map. Franklin Owen's expression, as he frowned at the unfinished drink in his hand, was abstracted and darkly troubled.

*　　*　　*

It was the tight schedule he was following that put the pressure on Dan Rawley—that, and a boisterous wind and heavy cloud ceiling that helped, at every moment, to remind him how close he was shaving the margin of time he had to work in. They were the reason he was allowing himself twenty-four hours in Denver. Taking any longer only meant increasing his gamble with the hurrying approach of winter.

He would have welcomed Frank Owen's offer to handle his cargo on consignment, except that it was essential that he have immediate cash. This meant that he had to deal with the matter himself, and he did, working through the camp and resolutely hunting out any buyer who could give him the kind of price he felt he had to have. He was even tempted to sell his wheel team, when one man made him an offer for the half-wild mules that he knew he couldn't duplicate. But in the end he turned it down, because he needed the assurance of a fast return to the Missouri. Time was as valuable to him now as money.

Close to midnight, Dan climbed the stairs to

97

the hotel room he shared with Hobie Drake, and when he got the lamp burning found his partner stretched out on the bed asleep, fully clothed except for his boots. Hobie woke and sat up, yawning and scratching yellow beard stubble. 'Everything under control? I was beginning to wonder if you meant to get any sleep tonight.'

Drugged tiredness made Dan's movements jerky and wooden as he hooked a pair of saddlebags over the back of a chair and tossed his hat and coat on top of them. He let a nod answer the question. Dropping onto the edge of the bed, he stared at his scuffed boots as though trying to summon the energy to pull them off.

Hobie said, 'You better lie down before you fall down—that is, if you're really set on pulling out of here at daylight. I been down and gave the wagon and the mules a last check-out. Everything's ready to go. And, there's this.' From his shirt pocket he took a crumpled piece of paper. He unfolded it and handed it over, so Dan could read his graceless scrawl. 'Your passenger list. The dust and coin is on the washstand, yonder.' He watched his partner's face a trifle uneasily, as the latter scanned the half dozen names.

Dan stopped and raised a frowning look above the paper's edge. 'Why is it you didn't collect from this fellow Tuthill? The deal was to be cash in advance.'

98

Hobie Drake cleared his throat. 'Dan, I want to tell you about Joe Tuthill. He's only a kid, not much more'n twenty. Last spring he brought his wife out from Indiana, and had to leave her in Kansas City because she was fixing to have a baby. He come on to the mines alone, figuring to hit it big—you know, a kid's wild ideas.

'Instead he lost everything; he hasn't a dime. And now there's word his wife and baby have been took sick. Dan, he's desperate!' Hobie drew a long breath. 'He promised if we'd take him, he'd do the cooking, and all the camp chores, and take care of the mules—anything at all, to pay his way. Dan, I couldn't turn him down! If you'd of been there, to hear him tell his story—'

'Damn it!' The cry broke from Dan Rawley, a hoarse outburst of fury that left his partner blinking. 'Do you think we can hand out charity?' He struck the piece of paper with the back of his hand. 'I was counting on every cent of that money!'

Hobie Drake stiffened; his gaunt cheeks turned slowly red. 'Sorry. I didn't suppose—'

But Dan rode over him, his own voice trembling with weariness and anger. 'I carry this whole enterprise on my own shoulders. I spend the day haggling to try and squeeze a miserable dollar or two extra out of the stuff in the wagon—and you turn around and do something like this to me! Seems as though, when I give you a job, you could at least try to get it right!'

That brought Hobie to his feet. He stood by the bed, glaring at his friend with bony hands clenched tight. Suddenly, he swung away to stand before the window, looking blindly out at a starless blackness that was broken by the barrel flares and windowlamps of Denver City.

'By God, you've really changed, haven't you!' he blurted finally. 'Nothing or nobody counts at all, so long as you make this business pay! It don't sound much like the Dan Rawley I used to think I knew.'

'Doesn't it?' His partner's voice was crisp, his level stare without warmth as Hobie turned back from the window.

'Hell, no! *He* wouldn't have turned his back on somebody in trouble, simply because it might cut his profits by a dollar or two! I'm beginning to wonder: Could be we both been wrong, from the beginning—about this whole thing. Maybe I just ain't mean enough to make a businessman, not if this is what it does to you. Maybe you don't really want somebody like me for a partner!'

The words hung heavy in the stillness of the hotel room. Slowly, then, Dan Rawley folded up the paper and shoved it into a pocket of his shirt. When he spoke the brittle anger was missing from his voice.

'If you really want out I won't try to hold you. But we're both dog-tired, and saying things we don't intend. Let it go, for now at least. Since you gave your word, we'll take this Joe Tuthill fellow with us tomorrow, on his terms. We could damn well have used his fare. Still, I reckon we'll manage. At the moment, I think we better try to get us some sleep.'

'Sure,' Hobie Drake said gruffly, his manner chastened. He hesitated, tried again. 'I'm sorry for what I said, Dan. I know what you got riding on your shoulders. I don't guess I meant some of that.'

'That's up to you,' Dan Rawley answered with a shrug. 'I'm willing to forget it if you are.' But it was a question whether things that had been aired, in such angry moments, could ever really cease to stand between them.

CHAPTER EIGHT

A raw wind pummeled Water Street, swinging signboards and fitfully whipping the barrel flares. The wind had driven most of Bellport's life indoors, until the town lay as empty and silent as the docks where the river sucked and gurgled sullenly at the pilings. No sternwheeler rode at a tie-rope's end tonight; the season was all but over, the River too low for safe navigation and too close to freeze-up. Bellport was nearly ready to batten down and prepare to tough out the long, dragging winter.

Wesley Boyd had the warped boardwalk to himself, only the strike of his own heels cutting across the moan of the wind. When he turned in at Milligan's, he found the saloon was little more than half full. At the bar he ordered whisky, slapping his money down with an angry gesture and throwing the liquor into him in the eager hope of putting its warmth through his chilled body. He didn't like Milligan's inferior stock and he grimaced at his own red-whipped features, reflected in the bar mirror. His eyes moved on then, seeking out his usual table. Vern Merrick was already seated in the accustomed place, bottle and glasses and rack of chips at his elbow. He was laying out a spread of solitaire as though oblivious to everything going on around him.

Merrick glanced up only when Wes Boyd pulled out the chair opposite. The eyes in the ravaged face met Boyd's with scarcely more than a flicker of greeting. 'You feel lucky tonight, my friend?' the gambler said.

Boyd dropped into the chair he always occupied. 'That's the hell of it,' he muttered. 'I always *feel* lucky!' He looked at the empty glass in his hand, as though surprised to find he had brought it over from the bar with him. Merrick saw the look, and moved the bottle closer. Boyd, who had told himself he would go easy with his drinking tonight and see if that had any effect on his luck, shrugged and picked up the bottle and poured himself a shot.

The other man was gathering up the cards with the disciplined grace of long practice. As his hands worked, the gambler's lusterless stare ranged the half-filled room. 'Not much action.'

'You think this is dead?' Boyd demanded, sourly. 'Wait a week or two. The only thing I know worse than a Kansas summer is the winters. Damned, hopeless backside of creation!'

'The evening is young,' Merrick said blandly. The cards blurred and whispered between his hands, as he deftly shuffled. 'Somebody ought to be showing up. Try a little two-handed showdown while we wait?'

'That's too fast a way to lose your money,' Wes Boyd objected. But then he lifted a shoulder, and tossed off his drink. 'Hell. Go on and deal them. My luck has *got* to change.'

He was reaching into a pocket for his leather cigar case when someone loomed beside him, bearing the chill of the outdoors on his clothing. Wes Boyd lifted an irritated glance, letting it run up the man's travel-stained shape to the lantern-jawed face. He scowled, and with a grin that showed the glint of strong white teeth, Hobie Drake said, 'Evening, Boyd. I'm here to collect on our bet.'

It took the other a moment to remember. 'Well!' he grunted. 'You actually made it, did you? And that partner of yours?'

'Naturally we made it. Cleared a good profit, too. We just got in about an hour ago—I hurried over because I knew you'd be anxious to hear.'

'Thanks!' Boyd said dryly. He turned away, then looked up irritably as he found the yellow-haired man still standing by his chair. 'Well—what do you want?'

Hobie Drake explained blandly, 'Why, for you to step to the bar and tell Milligan it's okay to pay over the stakes he's holding.'

'Oh.' With an impatient shrug, Boyd pushed back his chair and rose. 'Come along, then.'

He had to wait impatiently while the Irishman gave Hobie a rousing welcome. Then Hobie Drake, throwing his arm around the shoulders of a young tow-headed fellow who stood awkwardly by, hauled him to the bar for an introduction. 'And this here is Joe Tuthill—come back with us from the mines. Got him a sick wife and kid waiting in Kansas City. As fine a fellow as you ever met—but I never ate such terrible cooking!'

Young Tuthill flushed, grinning. And then Wes Boyd broke in, testily, reminding Drake of their business. 'I almost forgot,' Hobie told the Irishman. 'Mr. Boyd's anxious to see me get what I won off him. Whatever they tell you, he's a right generous fellow!'

Milligan brought out the stakes that he'd been holding in a canvas sack in his coin box. He counted out the stack of gold eagles. Hobie

104

spun one back to him across the wood, loudly ordering drinks for the crowd in celebration of his winning. After that the house must needs stand a round, but Wes Boyd managed to break away and return to his table, scowling and irritable.

Drawing young Tuthill out of the crowd around the bar, Hobie Drake pressed a couple of the gold coins into his hand. 'Now you can't go to your wife with empty pockets,' he said firmly when the young fellow started to protest. 'I want you to get yourself a room tonight, and a good meal. And in case I don't see you before you leave in the morning, remember I expect to be kept in the know about how things go for your wife and kid. Come spring, if you need a job look me up; I'll try to help you find one. Something that don't involve cooking!' he added, making a face.

Joe Tuthill was blinking hard and his mouth trembled. 'You been awful good to me,' he blurted. 'Mr. Rawley, too. I dunno what I'd done, if—if you hadn't—' Suddenly he grabbed Hobie's hand in both of his, squeezed it tightly, and went hurrying out. The big fellow stood and watched the street door slam behind him. Hobie's grin broke across his face; but then it slowly faded. 'Mr. Rawley, too,' he muttered under his breath, and his expression turned sour.

But he shook his head, dismissing the thought of his partner's contrariness. The remaining hoard of gold pieces demanded his attention. He had never possessed this much money at one time, and as he stood weighing the coins in his palm, something drew his eyes to the table where Wes Boyd sat facing the gambler. Deliberately, he turned and threaded his way over there.

Both men glanced up as he pulled out a chair for himself. Wes Boyd's face drew into a scowl. 'How about some fresh blood here?' Hobie suggested blandly. And he tossed several gold pieces onto the baize cloth, where they rolled and chimed together.

'Why not?' Merrick said as Boyd started to protest. 'It's an open game.' He pulled back the cards he had already commenced to deal. Hobie, enjoying the scowl on Wes Boyd's face, slacked into the chair and dropped his sweat-stained hat onto the floor beneath it. He shoved the double eagles at Merrick, stacked the chips that the gambler, as banker, passed him in return.

Merrick squared the deck for the cut. He won, and began to shuffle.

Hobie Drake was the most obnoxious type of poker player—the garrulous kind who could never seem to stop talking. His unceasing barrage of words plainly irritated Wes Boyd, and Hobie proceeded to work on him; but all the while his real attention was on every move that Vern Merrick made. He began to have an impression the gambler was feeling him out, deciding just how difficult it was going to be to separate him from that stack of gold coins. Soon this became a certainty that the man was employing a definite, if limited, repertoire of tinhorn tricks on him.

Hobie played along with it, still volubly talking, apparently not noticing as he let Merrick take a string of small pots. But he refused to rise to the bait by betting when he was dealt a hand that looked suspiciously enticing. It was Wes Boyd, playing recklessly as though distracted by the chatter, who filled out most of the pots Merrick drew in.

Once when the latter quit the table briefly, Hobie looked at Wes Boyd's dwindling supply of chips and said pleasantly, 'He seems to be getting into you. I'd say poker maybe ain't your game.'

Boyd's fist clenched tight. Through set lips he gritted, 'Don't you ever stop talking?'

Hobie's mocking grin was all the answer he got.

It was a few hands later that Hobie decided the time had come to put an end to this business. Boyd had given him a couple of small pairs, good enough to serve. 'Let's make this one interesting,' he said roughly, and playing Merrick expertly he raised and was raised again, keeping the betting going until Wes Boyd swore angrily and threw in his hand.

'It's you and me, friend,' Hobie told the gambler then. 'Let's see how brave you are!'

107

He shoved the rest of his chips into the pot, and tossed three double eagles after them. 'That's the works. That's all I got. It'll cost you that if you want to see my hand.'

Vern Merrick's eyes probed at him, narrowly, then studied his own cards. He folded them, tapped them thoughtfully on the table, passed them back and forth and from one hand to the other while he considered. For once his cool professional sureness seemed shaken; he drew the handkerchief from the breast pocket of his coat and carefully wiped his face, laid down his cards while he used the cloth on both palms and then replaced it. He picked the cards up and again considered them.

Calmly enough, he raised his stare to meet his challenger's. 'I'll call that,' he said, 'and I'll bump you a hundred. Sorry, friend, but you'll have to raise that much somewhere if you want to see what I'm holding.'

Hobie watched the lean hands drop the chips onto the table. 'Freezing me out, huh?' he said, sounding completely unconcerned. Turning in his chair he sent a shout across the room, then, that caused other voices to still. 'Milligan, how's my credit?'

The Irishman, placing a bristling handful of dripping beer schooners on the bar, answered, 'Try me, and see.'

'I got a hand that won't lose. I need a hundred to play it.'

Without hesitation, Milligan nodded his bald head. 'You got your hundred.'

In a quiet that made the creaking of the barrel chair a startling explosion, Hobie Drake turned back to his opponent. 'You're called.'

Merrick let a sneer touch his lips. 'You and your Irish friend may both regret it,' he said, and laid down four kings.

Hobie looked at them without batting an eye. When he lifted his head all trace of amusement was missing; his stare and his voice were level and utterly cold.

'I'm not calling *that* hand. I mean to have a look at the one in your pocket.'

The room seemed to hold its breath. Without seeming hasty, and so deliberately that Merrick didn't appear to think of stopping him, Hobie Drake reached for and caught the end of the hankerchief in the gambler's breast pocket; at his jerk its fold opened and everyone saw the five red-backed playing cards that came tumbling out, to scatter on the table.

Someone swore. As though galvanized by the sound, Vern Merrick moved; his right hand lifted convulsively.

Hobie was quicker. His own hand descended on the gambler's arm, twisting it and slamming it, hard, upon the table's edge. The derringer must have come out of the man's sleeve. Before he had his grip firmly set, it was wrenched from his fingers and spilled into the scatter of colored poker chips.

Merrick tried to grab for it with his free hand, but Hobie Drake scooped it up and pointed the weapon straight at its owner's face. He said, 'I think this takes the pot for me. What do *you* think?'

Merrick's breath was ragged and shallow in his throat, but he made no answer, merely glared as Hobie Drake leaned for the hat under his chair, placed it upside down in his lap and, left-handed, scooped coins and chips into it from the center of the table. The screech of chairlegs on rough boards was loud in the continuing stillness, as he pushed back from the table. Hobie cocked a look, askance, at Wes Boyd who was staring in dumb consternation at the man Hobie had exposed.

'He's not only a crook,' Hobie said, 'but a clumsy one. If you owe him any money, I don't think I'd worry too much about paying.'

Boyd only moved the palm of a hand, shakily, across his bearded face. Hobie stood, holding the hat. He looked at the derringer in his hand, tossed it contemptuously on the table in front of Merrick. 'I never had no use for a stingy gun.' He saw the fingers of Merrick's right hand twitch and actually make a slight move toward the weapon's inviting handle; but though he could read murder in the man's stare he calmly turned his back.

He knew what the crowd would do to Merrick if the latter actually tried to use the gun.

110

Men moved aside as he walked away to the bar; a murmur of voices and shuffling of feet began behind him. Hobie Drake ignored it all. He set his hat on the wood and told Milligan, 'Cash me in. And I wouldn't let that fellow in here again, if it was my place.'

'Don't worry!' the Irishman assured him, as he emptied the hat and began to count and stack the chips. 'I see him caught cheating one more time—out he goes!' He paid Hobie, withholding the house percentage.

Stuffing bills and coins into his pockets, Hobie turned and saw Nate Archer standing alone at the bar, a glass of whisky in front of him. He gave his former boss a wide grin. 'Too bad you don't believe in gambling, Nate,' he said pleasantly. 'You can see it pays off real good sometimes!'

The freighter merely looked at him—a baleful glare of such ferocity that Hobie, walking away from it, thought he could almost feel it scorch the back of his coat. Amused, and yet somewhat startled, he thought as he drew on his hat and went into the windy darkness: Now what do you make of that? I never figured Nate Archer liked me much—but I didn't think he'd begrudge me a little luck in a card game!

Still, he was not apt to lose much sleep worrying about what Archer thought of him. But from here on, when Vern Merrick was around, he had suspicion it might be well to watch his back.

*   *   *

Dan Rawley was in his room at the boardinghouse, packing to leave, when a timid sound took him to the door where he found Bud Crocker with hand lifted to knock again. Dan could only stare at him. 'Why—hello, Bud. Whatever are you doing here? Come in.'

'Please, sir.' Even under the pain stress of anxiety, Bud remembered his manners. 'I been hunting all over town for you. Ma sent me. It's Mister Drake—he's been hurt.'

'Hurt! How?'

'Somebody tried to kill him!'

'They *what*?' Quickly Dan turned to get hat and windbreaker off the bed, and blow out the light. 'I'm right with you,' he said bleakly. 'You tell me about it.'

But the youngster knew little, apparently, and Dan had to stem the rush of startled questions while they hurried across town through the early dusk, with a red stain of sunset lying flat among the south-west rim of flat Kansas sky. Meg Crocker lived in a tiny house at the edge of the business district, that she managed to keep neat and homelike for herself and her children, despite the poverty of its furnishings. As Dan and the boy entered, she came from the bedroom and her face was gray with shock; her voice, when she spoke, was drained of strength. 'Oh, thank God you're here!' To Bud she said, 'Your sister is next door. I want you to go there and stay till I call you. And I don't want to hear about either one of you making Mrs. Cooper any trouble.'

'No, ma'am.'

Obediently he left. The moment he was gone, the woman's shoulders slumped. Dan stepped quickly and guided her to a chair at the table that still held the clutter of a meal. 'Are you all right?' he demanded, anxiously.

She nodded, but her mouth trembled and her eyes shone now with unshed tears. 'It was the way it happened! Mister Rawley, the awful thing is we *quarreled*. Mister Drake's the finest man in the world—and yet I told him to get out of my house, that I never wanted to see him again.'

Dan waited, holding his impatience, sensing that she would have to tell this in her own way.

'I'd never seen him quite like he was this evening—I mean that moody and upset. I'm sure he'd been drinking. I thought maybe he was concerned over the two of you leaving again for Denver in the morning; but, it wasn't that. Then finally the real truth came out: It had to do with slavery!

'That's one thing we'd never discussed, Mister Rawley. I guess you know how—how my Sam was killed. By those abolitionists, down near Fort Scott?' When Dan nodded, she went on tonelessly: 'I suppose it's made me

113

unreasonable on the subject. But tonight, when Mister Drake started talking against the South—about what he hoped Abe Lincoln was going to do to the secessionists when he's elected next week, and how every slave holder was a devil—well, it just didn't sound like him! I am afraid I lost my head. We had some terrible words; I told him he'd better leave. And he went storming down the front walk, and—right out there at the street, they—they were waiting!'

'Who, Meg?'

She shook her head. 'I don't know. It was over so quickly. But, there were two of them. I saw it all from the doorway. I even saw the knife . . .'

'A knife!' Dan Rawley felt his blood run cold at the mere thought of it. 'How bad was he hurt? And where?'

'Just under the ribs—low, on the right side. They ran when I screamed so I guess they didn't have time to make sure of him. But I've had the doctor here, and he says it was an awful near thing. Oh, Mister Rawley . . .' Suddenly her mouth began to tremble and she pressed the knuckles of a hand against it.

Dan touched her shoulder, awkwardly. 'I'd like to see him.'

She nodded and, with face averted, got quickly to her feet. She went to the bedroom door for a look, then beckoned to him. Dan followed her in.

114

Hobie Drake lay on the sagging iron bed, a quilt drawn to his chin, head thrown back and eyes closed. To Dan he appeared to be scarcely alive as he breathed shallowly through a gaping mouth; under the low-turned lamp, his flesh looked waxen from the shock of the bandaged wound. But he was awake; his eyes wavered open and he whispered his partner's name.

Dan stepped to the bed and took one of the big hands in his own. 'I'm right here. How are you feeling?'

More of the quick, shallow breathing, before Hobie found strength to answer. 'Like a well-carved turkey!' He added, with an angry grimace, 'Fine thing for me to go and do—with us all set to pull out in the morning.'

'Don't worry about *that,*' Dan told him. 'I'll manage. And you shouldn't be trying to talk. Only—can you tell me who did it? That gambler you had the run-in with, maybe, the day we got in from Denver?'

Hobie shook his head on the pillow. 'Merrick? No, no—not him. I'd know this bird, all right, if I saw him again. He must live by the knife! Got him a cut somebody gave him— clean across his nose.' He gestured feebly, trying to point to his own face.

Dan Rawley, who could remember seeing no one of such description in Bellport, could only ask, 'Do you have any idea what he might have been after?'

'I reckon,' Hobie touched tongue to dry lips. 'I'm spitting cotton. Could I have a drink of water?'

'A very small one,' Meg Crocker said. 'You heard the doctor say to be careful.' There was a tumbler on the table by the bed. Dan stood out of the way as she moved over to lift his head and hold the glass for Hobie to moisten his lips and tongue. Even that small movement left him gasping as she lowered him to the pillow again.

'Good girl, Meg,' he panted. He added: 'Now, if you'll leave me and Dan alone for a minute . . .'

She frowned in puzzlement, but offered no argument. She even closed the door behind her so the two could be alone. Hobie's eyes followed her out, then lifted again to his friend's face. 'A fine woman, Dan. We had a row—did she tell you? I'm ashamed, but, there's things weighin' on my mind.'

Dan was completely in the dark. 'I don't understand. She said the argument had to do with slavery.'

Either Hobie was feeling stronger, or he called on hoarded resources. 'That's what I had to tell you . . . I guess you never knew, I got friends with the Railroad.'

Dan stared. 'You mean—the Underground?'

'That's right. Running slaves north out of Missouri and Arkansas, along the Kansas border. I even took a batch through one time, my own self, when there was an emergency. Well—there's another emergency.'

'How do you mean?'

'One of the couriers—he drives a peddler's wagon for a cover—he ran into trouble last week, with a couple of Southern slave hunters chasing him. He had a man in his wagon and he tried to shake them by swinging west, went as far out of his way as the Big Blue crossing. He had to leave his cargo there, with the ferryman, so he could turn back. The ferryman's still got it hid and he wants shut of it.'

Dan began to think he saw the shape of what was coming and he stiffened. His mouth settled and hardened. He said crisply, 'You're going to tell me your friends looked you up, to ask us to help take a runaway slave off their hands!'

The hurt man's eyes, dulled with pain, clung to his. 'Dan, it's desperate or they wouldn't even have suggested it! If the other side gets to that ferryman, and makes him tell what he knows—the whole damn setup could bust open. They knew we were goin' out tomorrow. They give me the password, said if we could pick up the cargo and run it to Fort Kearney, they got somebody at Dobytown who'll take delivery.'

He lifted a hand, clutched at his partner's sleeve. 'Dan, I told them exactly how you'd feel. After that business about Joe Tuthill, I knew you'd want nothing to do with anything like this that might endanger getting the wagon to Denver. But they made me promise I'd ask.' He had half raised his head from the pillow. He dropped back, and his face was wet with sweat and lined with pain. 'So, I asked. Now let's say we forget it.'

'Let's say we do,' Dan Rawley agreed bluntly, to dispose of the matter.

Yet, as he looked at his partner's face, it angered him that for some senseless reason he should find himself feeling suddenly guilty, and on the defensive.

CHAPTER NINE

The ferry at the Big Blue crossing was a clumsy-looking raft of logs running on a cable that stretched from bank to bank. One might have thought, at first glance, it would be hardly enough to support a loaded wagon and team against the river's current. But Dan Rawley knew it well, and its capacities. As he came toward the landing with a load of perishables in the wagon bed behind him—barrels of flour and eggs and apples, salt pork packed between layers of shelled corn, and other produce he knew would bring a top price in the mining camps—he wasn't worried about getting his

118

cargo safely across. It was another matter entirely that turned his face grave with concern, and filled him with caution.

Rolls of sooty cloud pressed lumpishly against the earth. It had been raining since mid-morning, and in a lashing wind the spears of rain rattled on the wagon canvas and the roof of the ferry buildings and the dock, hissed in the bare branches of stripped trees along the bank. He saw no one about, at first. The ferry lay against the near dock and smoke rose from the stovepipe chimney, battered by the storm. Now a door opened and the ferryman stepped out, shrugging into his windbreaker. He was a skinny, stoop-shouldered man named Pittman. When he recognized his customer, some of the cautious tightness seemed to smooth away from about his eyes.

'Running kind of late, ain't you?' he grunted. 'Where's that other feller?'

'My partner's been laid up.' Dan added, 'Don't you generally close down before now?'

The ferryman admitted it. 'Damn little business, this late in the season.'

Shuffling his feet against the chill, he looked away from Dan, running a searching look along the timber lining the sullen slide of the river. His whole manner spelled uneasiness and fear, and it was an impulse of curiosity that made Dan speak the words he hadn't intended to—using the password Hobie Drake had told him: 'I suppose you don't see many of

119

the right kind of people . . .'

Pittman's head seemed to jerk. Slowly his eyes slid back to Dan's. Suspicion and sharp disbelief faded in them as he probed Dan's face. His narrow chest swelled on a drawn breath and when he spoke his voice shook, as though with relief. 'Come inside!' he said roughly, and turned to lead the way.

Dan anchored the reins and, still wondering what had prompted him, climbed down to follow him into the shack. It was as dismal as its location on the mud bank of the crossing— half soddy and half milled lumber, under a musty-smelling dirt roof laid over boards. The ferryman lived alone, and he had only the one room with a bunk, a rusted stove, a homemade table and chairs and a packing box nailed to the wall for a cupboard. There was very little light on a dismal winter day.

As Dan entered, he heard table legs scraping the floor; Pittman turned from shoving his table over against the wall, and said tersely, 'Shut the door, and drop the bar!' That done, he leaned and hooked his fingers under the edge of a trap door in the crude plank flooring, and swung it up and back. 'All right,' he said, into the dank hole beneath. 'You can come out of there!'

For a moment, silence. Then a wooden ladder creaked, and a head in the broken wreckage of a hat appeared. The head tilted back; smoky eyes in a black face peered up at them. Pittman said impatiently, 'It's all right—this is the man you've been waiting for.'

The black man bobbed his head and, without a word, clambered out of the hole. He was dressed in a filthy shirt and pants and threadbare jacket; the leather of his shapeless workshoes was badly split. Yet shivering with cold there seemed to be a natural dignity about him.

Shocked, Dan scowled at Pittman as he demanded, 'You haven't been keeping him in that hole?'

'Only put him there when I hear somebody coming,' the ferryman said righteously. 'What do you think I am? I been taking real good care of him. Gave him food, and a place to sleep.' He pointed; Dan saw, now, the pile of sacks and old blankets in the corner by the stove. 'And, by God, I'm glad to be rid of him! This ain't in my line!'

'Mine either,' Dan started to say; but Pittman was too full of his own troubles.

'It's been the longest week I ever lived through! Waiting to get caught, and likely end up hanging from one of them trees out there.' He shook his head. 'I'd never do it again, for any man! Soon as you clear out of here with him, I'm closing this place down and getting the hell out of here for Lawrence for the winter.'

'Now, wait!' Dan began. 'I didn't say—' But then he saw the futility of setting the man

121

straight. Pittman had worn out his nerve, and you plainly could not put any more on him. Well, then, he thought sourly, for Hobie's sake?

He drew a breath and looked at the colored man who stood motionless before them. 'What's your name?'

'Joe's the only name they ever gave me,' the man said

'All right, Joe. You go out and climb in back of the wagon. You'll find some blankets there. Make yourself as comfortable as you can—and keep out of sight.'

The ferryman said quickly: 'Wait! Let me check, first.' At the door, he took down the bar and stepped out into the rain. He was gone for a couple of minutes. He stuck his head in again to say, 'The coast is clear; at least, I don't see nobody. Get him in that rig, mister—and take him the hell away from here!'

When Dan resumed his place on the wagon's seat, Pittman was already at the ferry slip waiting, in a frenzy of haste now, to bring him aboard and pole him across. There was no sign of the Negro, who had wasted no time in burrowing into the back of the wagon. Even when Dan spoke across his shoulder, saying, 'You all set?' he got no answer. He shrugged and, squared around on the seat, yelled his mules down the dip of the mud bank to where the ferry bobbed in cold, sliding water.

At length the rain ended, leaving the prairie

sodden and steaming beneath the heavy cloud ceiling. Dan Rawley got down to go around checking the lashings of his canvas. At the rear he heard movement inside and he called softly, 'All right, in there?' Not sure he got an answer, he pulled the canvas back and discovered the colored man, huddled into a blanket that he clutched about him. 'You managing to keep warm?'

Dan saw then that his passenger was shaking with the cold. But he managed a nod. 'Doin' just fine,' he said.

Frowning, Dan studied the man. 'I don't imagine it gets like this much, the part of the world where you're from.'

Despite his misery, the other managed to grin briefly, showing startlingly white teeth. 'Not Louisiana, no sir.'

'Well, hang on a while longer and we'll be making camp. A fire, and some hot grub ought to fix you up.'

Out of consideration, Dan camped earlier than he normally would; even so, the weather brought the day to a hasty close and it was full dark before they had the mules on picket, and a fire making its single golden break against the vastness of the wet night. Joe helped, handling the animals, in a way that suggested he had a natural knack with them. Later he huddled close to the fire, soaking up its warmth and working at the plate of food Dan dished up for him.

Hungry enough himself, Dan Rawley found himself giving less attention to the food than to the person across the fire from him. A Northern man, Dan had read *Uncle Tom's Cabin* and had seen some glimpses of slavery in Missouri; but this was the first time he had had any close experience with one of its victims from the real Deep South. He asked suddenly, 'How does it feel to know you belong to another man, just like you were a horse or a mule?'

The black man only looked at him, and finally had to shake his head. 'Might be easier to answer if I'd ever known anything else!'

'Were you badly treated?'

'No sir. Can't say I was. For near ten years, I had me a real fine master. He bought me when I was a young sprout and made me his personal servant. He was good to me. Even taught me things—how, to sign my name, and to read some.' He shot Dan a look, over his coffee cup. 'Maybe you don't know, they got laws against that—teaching a black man to read. You ain't supposed to teach him nothing!'

Dan's eyes narrowed. 'I always heard the only excuse for slavery was that it helped take savages out of the jungle and bring them to civilization.'

The other grimaced, and looked into his cup. 'Yes sir. Seems to me I heard that, too.'

Silence lay upon them, broken by the

124

crackle of flames and the whine of the night wind, and the stirring of the mules on their tethers. After a moment, still pursuing the subject, Dan Rawley remarked, 'And you ran away? From this man who'd risked breaking the law to help you have an education?'

'Oh, no sir—not from him. He always said, when he died, I was to have my freedom—me, and my wife and baby too. I swear it's the truth, sir! Only, he was took too sudden. He left a lot of debts behind, and everything sort of broke up. All of us servants got sold off, real quick. My wife and child went down the river to Mississippi. A man from Arkansas come and took me to settle what was owed him.' Joe hesitated. His voice harshened. 'He wasn't like Old Master. He was a whippin' man.'

Dan exclaimed, 'And they really broke up your family? I guess I knew that kind of thing happened . . .'

'Yes sir.' There was a sudden break in the man's voice—as though, for all his stoical fortitude, the wound was still too fresh, the ache too strong. 'Don't reckon I'm apt to see 'em again, ever. Though maybe, if I was free . . .'

His head lifted, the whites of his eyes shining in the fireglow. 'Old Master let me look at a map, once, and I got it to memory just in case. So I remembered where Arkansas was if I could just start north and west from there, and somehow keep going, I might get to my freedom.

'The second time New Master whipped me, I took off. The dogs almost got me a couple times. Then these white men found me, who said they was part of the Underground and they'd help me get away. I thought sure they was lying; but they've took me this far and now here you are—troubling yourself on account of me. Why?' He peered at Dan in earnest puzzlement. 'Why would any white man do this?'

Thinking by what a narrow chance he happened to be doing it at all, Dan could give no good answer. He shrugged and set aside his emptied plate. 'We're both men, aren't we?' he said gruffly.

'All I know,' the other told him fiercely, a fist clenching, 'I've got the taste of freedom in my mouth and I just ain't gonna spit it out again. I can't. They'll have to kill me first!' He leaned closer. 'You know, I been hearing tell of a man they call Lincoln. Down there, the white folks talk about nothing else much. They say he's agin slavery. They're all scared to death maybe he's gonna do something to get rid of it. What do you think, mister?'

Such eagerness and hope seemed to Dan, just then, somehow pathetic—tragic, even. It wouldn't do, trying to explain what he had learned about the differences between campaign oratory and political expedience; or voicing his own reservations as to how much this fellow, Lincoln, could accomplish if he tried to move against Southern institutions, instead of merely making fine speeches about no house being able to stand divided against itself.

So, needing to make some answer, he simply shrugged and said lamely, 'Well— maybe.' And then his head lifted sharply and he flung up a warning hand.

The other's reaction showed that he, too, had heard the rider coming toward their campfire at a walk. Joe started to his feet, tin cup and plate spilling, but it was already too late to reach a hiding place. Dan shook his head at him as he eased to a stand, right hand pushing the skirt of his coat away from his holster.

After that, the rider was entering the circle of firelight and he reined up, the horse under him blowing a jet of steam from each nostril into the frosty air.

The man was a bulky figure, in the folds of a heavy winter coat, face shadowed by a hat brim. He placed both hands on the saddlehorn. If he read anything in Dan Rawley's manner, he gave no sign of it. He said, pleasantly enough, 'I was glad to see your fire. It's a bitter night for traveling.'

'You look to be traveling pretty light,' Dan commented, indicating the lack of any sort of pack.

'Heading up the trail to the next stage station,' the other answered. 'I guess it's further than I thought.' He made a move to dismount, checked it as he looked to Dan for permission. 'Do you mind?'

Trail courtesy took precedence over mere suspicion. Reluctantly, Dan shook his head. 'No. Step down—make yourself comfortable. There's beans and coffee.'

'I can smell 'em.' Leather popped as the man swung off. 'Nothing harder than a cold saddle,' he observed pleasantly, stomping the stiffness from his legs. As he did, he turned his head and Dan sensed that the eyes in the still-unseen face were moving about—checking the camp, the wagon, the mules staked out. Finally the man looked at Joe but passed him by without comment. Instead, turning again to Dan, he asked, 'Freighter?'

Dan Rawley nodded. 'On a small scale.'

'Takes nerve, this time of year,' the stranger observed, and dropped the subject. He was advancing toward the fire now, mittened hands extended to embrace its warmth. 'That feels damned good!' he murmured. Standing at the fire, he used a thumb to push the hat back upon his forehead—and now Dan saw his face in the glow of the wind-whipped flames.

It would have been a very ordinary face, except for the slash of a knife blade in someone's strong hand which had, at some previous time, broken the profile of the nose, smashing it as it carved its way straight across his face.

Seeing the man who had stabbed Hobie Drake, Dan let the breath from his lungs in an explosion of pale steam. Then he was grabbing for his holster again, but the skirt of his coat was in his way and he fought it aside and his fingers were closing on the chill gun butt.

A voice behind him said, 'Careful! Just take it out and throw it down!'

Every muscle in Dan Rawley's back went right. For that moment he couldn't have moved, whether to turn or duck or run. He heard a pistol snick to full cock; a boot sole scraped grittily. Slowly and cautiously, then, Dan forced his fingers to lift the gun from his belt holster, and let it fall. Immediately, someone closed in on him from the dark. A gun's muzzle jabbed his ribs. A boot toe struck the fallen pistol and sent it spinning away across freezing mud.

Dan eyed his two captors, coldly furious at letting himself be taken so easily—the one man riding in boldly, keeping him engaged with talk so his companion could come in from the other side and catch him by surprise. The scarred man was grinning now, the lifting of the cheeks warping the knife-gash and making his face seem all the more hideous. 'Very good,' he said, nodding to the prisoner. 'We want you alive. Up to now, we ain't had much luck. We had to kill the ferryman. But, from what you're going to tell us—names and places—you're going to help us rout out the

129

whole Kansas branch of that damned Nigra-stealin' Underground!'

Coldly Dan said, 'I don't know anything to tell, if I wanted to.'

At once a blow on the side of the head staggered him. The man with the gun said harshly, 'Don't worry, Nigra-lover! We're gonna make you want to!'

Dan caught his footing, saved himself from going down. As he waited silently for his head to clear, he saw the one with the scar-face turn again to look at Joe. 'And you know what's going to happen to *you*, boy—you that likes to run? We know what to do with runnin' Nigras!'

A step took the man to his horse, to burrow into a saddlebag. There was a glint of metal in firelight, a clink of chain, and he held up an ugly-looking set of shackles and leg-irons. 'All right, you!' He beckoned to Joe with a crooking finger. 'Come over and get these on, hear?'

Dan Rawley, helplessly watching, could sense the despair in the runaway as he stared at the shackles swaying in his captor's hand—the hated symbols of his bondage, from which he had had his brief liberty. When he failed to move, the scarred man, with a savage curse, reached and got him by the shoulder.

The touch, and the irons shoved into his face, broke the spell of authority. A wordless cry broke from the black man and he went suddenly berserk, shaking free of the grip on his shoulder, batting at the shackles to shove them away. The scarred man, cursing, swung the irons like a flail. Dan saw one of the heavy leg-irons strike Joe full in the face, saw the bright spurt of blood. But Joe refused to cringe away like a whipped animal, instead without warning, he leaped full upon his enemy, work-hardened fingers reaching for the throat. They collided and fell together, and the scarred man lost his grip on the shackles and dropped them with a clatter.

The second one, breaking loose from surprise, yelled and started forward. It gave Dan Rawley his chance. A hard downward chop with the edge of a palm against the man's arm failed to dislodge the gun, but did deflect it; and then Dan's other fist took him in the chest and set him staggering. The man cried out and fired almost by reflex, muzzle flash smearing the darkness.

Empty-handed against a weapon, Dan jerked away and sought the glimmer of his own pistol, lying where the other's boot had kicked it. Desperately, he took a running plunge and dived at the weapon, lungs clamped tight in expectation of another shot and the shock of a bullet. He hit hard, at full length. He found the gun, but the wet handle nearly squirted from his fingers. He trapped it, and was rolling as he scooped it up—and as that other gun spoke and spattered him with chips of gouted mud and ice. Flat on his back in icy water, Dan saw

131

his enemy targeted against the fire, and he shot and shot again. Afterward, half-blinded by the flashes and deafened by the explosions, he held his hand as the black silhouette bent slowly forward and dropped in a twisting fall.

Dan seemed unable to move at all, for a count of three; then he became aware of Joe and the other white man, locked in a desperate embrace, and he lifted himself onto an elbow. Strange, savage sounds came from the struggling pair yonder. The black man, he saw now, had both hands at his enemy's throat, in a convulsive grip. Pinned down, the other was frantically thrashing and writhing under Joe's weight.

But there was something, Dan thought in a daze, that had slipped his mind—something he should remember . . . Then it came to him, and as he rolled to his knees, Dan was shouting. 'Joe: Look out! *He has a knife!*'

The warning was too late. Even as he lunged toward them, still clutching the smoking pistol, he saw the sudden thrust of the white man's arm—the convulsive answering arch of Joe's back. Again, and yet a third time, the vicious jab was repeated. But the runaway's fingers were locked in place and no force could break them loose. The white man's head was bent far back now, the scarred face hideously twisted.

Suddenly Joe went limp. As though of their own accord, now that their work was done, the black fingers clutching his opponent's throat relaxed; Joe's head sagged sideward. Leaning, Dan put a hand on his shoulder and rolled him off his dead enemy—and saw the knife sunk to its hilt, and the blood. He stood stunned.

So Joe would never make it to freedom; but his hunger for it had kept his hands clamped on the throat of his enemy, even with that knife plunging again and again into his vitals. Shaken and yet deeply moved, Dan Rawley straightened slowly and ran a hand across his face and found it wet with sweat.

There was no tribute he felt capable of speaking—nothing more at all that he could do for this brave and cheated man—except to find a spade and scrape out some kind of grave in this empty, frozen prairie where he could be buried together with the two white enemies with whom he had died.

It was sometime toward mid-morning, and some dozen miles west of Kearney, that a rhythmic stitching of sound began to grow behind him, against the constant sough of the wind, and the noise of his own outfit. Dan Rawley pulled rein almost unconsciously, and stood on the wagon's seat so he could look back over the canvas of the hood. And there, where the broad trail broke the horizon, the lone rider suddenly topped into view.

On a stripped-down saddle, crouched for speed as he hurtled his pony across the empty miles, the express rider came with the mail pouches that helped bring the two halves of a continent together. Dan Rawley watched horse and man grow steadily in size, the pulse of flying hoofs beating louder off the twin sounding boards of earth and cloud ceiling. Then abruptly the rider was abreast of him, flashing by the halted wagon, without a pause or so much as an answering wave of the hand. Instead, a shout came drifting back across the hunched shoulder: *'Lincoln's elected!'*

He passed and was gone again. But Dan Rawley, all cynicism forgotten, was left whooping with excitement as he stood there on the wagon seat and scaled his hat toward the threatening sky.

CHAPTER TEN

The first bite of sleet, knifing at him beneath the edge of the canvas, was Dan Rawley's warning that real trouble had finally struck. So far—something like three days still out of Denver City—his luck had held. But the luck he'd boldly relied on from the start of this enterprise seemed very close, now, to being used up.

He knew it was the absence of Hobie Drake that spelled the difference. With Hobie along he estimated they would have made it with time to spare; alone, there had been delays and loss of hours which had finally added up and thrown him badly off schedule. Even so, until this moment, the winter had withheld its hand. But now he knew that one of those incredibly ferocious plains blizzards was just about to engulf him.

Another knife blade of sleet sliced down from the greasy-looking cloud ceiling, and then it was coming fast—rattling on the canvas, filling the chill day with a sibilant hissing. Dan tightened his grip on the reins as the mules began to act up in angry protest. Suddenly the air had turned densely white. Earth and horizon vanished, the fringe of scrub growth along the distant river bed withdrew behind a veil that shook and trembled in the rising wind. Ice pellets leaped and writhed like live things as they danced over bare ground and dead grass; then visibly the earth began to fade out into a uniform whiteness.

The teams had hafted, dead still in their tracks. When Dan yelled at them, the sound of his voice was blotted up. Using the whip, he got the wagon inching forward again, but the mules still balked at every step. The wind, growing fiercer, shifted erratically until it seemed almost to blow from every compass point at once, and Dan realized in alarm it was becoming really hopeless trying to set anything like a straight course. But instinct told him he must keep moving.

The sleet had turned to snow that began to blow over the ground in blinding streamers. It was now no more than the middle of afternoon, yet most of the light had already leaked out of the day, and night seemed almost to be falling. Soon every landmark, even the trail itself, was completely lost; Dan felt as though he were on a blind treadmill that was soundless except for this howling fury. He flipped up the collar of his windbreaker but, with his hands full managing the reins, could only duck his head against the occasional cross draft that came battering in at him beneath the forward bow, hitting him with a smother of snow crystals that seemed to suck the breath out of him.

Disaster, when it struck, gave no warning at all.

With visibility at zero, he had no hint of the near fall-off of the ground—knew nothing of it, until the near rear wheel dropped suddenly away from under him. Instantly, he was on his feet and yelling at the mules, trying to put them into their collars for a saving pull. It was futile. His shout was lost as the wagon quickly slewed round, dragged off kilter by its own weight. Dan felt the whole rear end begin to settle, the wagon box tilting at an ever wilder angle. Spiny brush lashed the canvas, the carefully loaded cargo shifted. And the rig started to go over.

He tried at the last moment to leap for

safety but he was too late, with nothing under him to give him purchase. He heard the squealing of the mules as they found themselves carried off their feet; then, in a complete tangle, wagon and teams were tumbling ponderously through brush and eroded rock. The wagon struck a boulder, went completely over in a crazy smashing of timbers. Dan Rawley's skull made crushing contact with something, and consciousness was wiped away.

A forlorn and agonized braying was in his ears when Dan roused. He lay for a moment, unable to remember just what had happened to him. This confusion passed but, even then, it seemed impossible to move. He was numbed, his brain seemingly unable to will life into his limbs.

Finally he stirred and rolled with an effort onto one elbow. Drifted snow cascaded from his clothing. Looking around, he saw that he must have been thrown clear as the wagon reached the bottom of its plunge. He lay at the bottom of a draw studded with boulders and spiny growth. The walls helped somewhat to break the wind's force, but snow was falling steadily. A dozen yards from him the smashed wreckage of the wagon lay beneath a mounding whiteness. Its canvas was tattered, its bows smashed. The spokes of one wheel had crumpled like matchsticks.

He saw the mules, now, standing unmoving

in a tangle of harness—all but one that was down and struggling with an obviously broken leg. He realized it was the tortured braying of the hurt animal that had helped to rouse him.

Stifling a groan, Dan Rawley came up out of the snowdrift; but when he tried to stand, he seemed unable to feel any part of him below his ankles. His legs gave way under him and sent him sprawling. After a moment he tried again, this time supporting himself against a boulder until he could get his feet to functioning. Staggering and lurching, he made his way over to the ruined wagon and clung to it while, through a clinging fog of his own breath, he surveyed the damage.

It was as bad as he could have imagined. The wagon was demolished, the cargo a total loss. Barrels of apples and eggs and corn and other foodstuffs were broken and smashed, disgorging their contents into the general wreckage. In this roaring winter wilderness, nothing could be salvaged. His investment, and the fruit of all his efforts, had been wiped out for him in a single, ruinous instant.

The hurt mule was still carrying on piteously. Dan Rawley hobbled over for a look at him, fumbling for the holster under his blanket coat as he saw the animal's condition. Only a quick bullet could do the beast any good. He got out his gun and made short work of it, his face bleak and his jaw set as the flat crack of the pistol shot was blotted up by the smothering storm.

Now he had to think about getting himself out of this predicament alive.

Still groggy, still far from trustful of his own thought processes, he made his way again to the wagon for a closer look at the tumbled mess that had been its contents. Poking around, he found his blanket roll but decided the shotgun must have been flung wide and sunk without a trace in the piling snowdrifts. He quickly gave up looking for it. There was nothing else worth salvaging, though he found a gunnysack and stowed a couple of the slabs of salt pork in it—unless he got to shelter, and soon, he thought he was rather more apt to freeze to death before he starved. He fashioned a crude pack to sling across his shoulders, leaving his hands free. Resolutely, then, he turned his back on this scene that mocked the wreckage of his business career.

Three of his mules remained on their feet. There was nothing he could do for a couple of them but cut them loose, to shift for themselves as best they might. That done, he turned to the third one which, he believed and hoped, was rather more tractable than the others. So far as he knew, the animal had never been ridden, with a saddle or without. He made friendly sounds as he approached, watching the waggling semaphores of the animal's ears and the wicked rolling of the suspicious eyes. Cautiously, he managed to

139

haul himself astride.

If the mule had wanted to remember it was a mule, there was not a thing in Dan's present condition that he could have done about it. He thoroughly expected to be slammed into a drift; but for a wonder, this mule seemed to sense that they were both in serious trouble and that the man on its back might know the way out. Dan felt the muscles stiffen and bunch and the deep barrel swell between his knees, but the beast stood steady and unmoving except for a single sideward swing of its head and a flash of yellow teeth. It expended its wind in a long shuddering breath, let its head drop again. Dan took a breath, and gingerly used his heels.

After a second cautious nudge, and a shout that came out as something more like a croak, he was rewarded by having his ungainly mount step slowly, grudgingly forward. It didn't like the wind but it responded to his pull on the halter. They came out of the coulee where they had cracked up, and Dan Rawley ducked his head as the full numbing force of the storm hit him.

Perhaps it was not snowing quite so hard, he thought, though he could see nothing but a monotonous, white sameness. The sun was lost beyond hope, somewhere behind the cloud ceiling. There was no landmark that meant anything. He could only assume the wind was holding steady from the north. If this guess

140

was correct, then keeping it against his right should bring him west and eventually to the Platte, from where he could take his bearings. If his guess was wrong, then the mistake could likely have only one outcome.

He quickly lost any sense of time or distance. It took all his effort to cling to his place, without saddle or stirrups, and with limbs that grew more and more devoid of feeling. He soon found it was impossible to keep the wind in the proper quarter—at any easing of his dragging pull on the halter, the plodding mule would swing away from it. Dan Rawley began after a while to believe it was a futile effort, anyway, for no sign of river bank growth or of any other recognizable landmark showed, even after what seemed like hours of struggling on in this way. Soon it was all he could do just to keep the animal moving.

Now it was too late, he saw the wise thing would have been to stay near the wreck where there'd been food, and a shelter of sorts, to get him through the storm. He must have been too dazed from that blow on the head to reason clearly . . .

*   *   *

He roused, to find himself in a still darkness. The day seemed completely gone. Strangely enough, so did the push and howl of the wind. In this odd quiet he had to concentrate even to feel the cold. Puzzled, Dan tried to boot the mule ahead but it stood rock-steady, utterly refusing to budge. Finally, with a groan of impatience, he threw his boot over and slid off into deep snow.

His numb right leg promptly buckled under him and threw him forward to his knees. One arm, flung out for balance, struck against something that felt exactly like a man-made wall. Not believing it, he knelt in the snow as he fumbled at his mitten, ripped it off with his teeth, and felt again. And this time, unmistakably, his searching fingers made out the neat layers of sod bricks. A building!

The discovery brought him to his feet to stumble blindly along the side of the structure, supporting himself against it and dragging the mule after him as he hunted for a door. He rather thought this must be a barn. He knew he was right when, moments later, he rounded a corner and saw the dim outline of a sod house, yards ahead of him, and light spilling about the edges of a shuttered window.

He put all his strength into a yell. A slab door was flung open, letting out a rush of lamplight past the man silhouetted in the opening. Dan Rawley yelled again, and stumbled blindly toward it.

*　　　*　　　*

Still limping from the frostbite that had

narrowly missed costing him a couple of toes, still a trifle shaky after two weeks in bed with something that had been diagnosed as very nearly pneumonia, Dan Rawley knew he was lucky even to be on his feet. He was lucky to be alive at all, in fact, and in Denver City—lucky for the freak of chance that had led his mule to that road ranch soddy near the Platte. By all odds, he should be lying underneath one of those drifts out on the sage flats, waiting God-knew-how-long for someone, someday, to stumble across his bones.

Nevertheless, it was hard to keep up one's courage and one's spirit, in face of total disaster. He was still too close to his loss and not yet far enough along in convalescense; he couldn't seem to find the resilience to bounce back from this defeat, and put his mind to alternatives and future plans. Today, as he walked into Frank Owen's store on F Street, it took an effort to return the merchant's cordial, cheerful greeting.

Owen was talking with a pair of men that Dan knew to be Hinton and McCabe, two of his associates. 'You're looking some better,' Owen commented, after making brief introductions. 'Thanks for coming in, Dan. I guess Whitledge won't be able to make it, but there's enough of us here to talk business. Let's go in the office.'

In the little room with the mining district map on the wall, they seated themselves and

Owen broke out a bottle and glasses, poured drinks all around. 'To success!' he offered. Dan drank with the others, though the irony of the toast put a wry quirk to his mouth. He was frankly puzzled at his being asked to come here.

Owen quickly got down to cases. 'Here's the situation. Me and my friends'—he indicated them with a nod—'we've decided on something we think is a pretty smart investment. If it ain't—well, maybe it's better to lose your shirt all at once, than just prolong the agony. Be that as it may, Dan, we've gone and pooled our credit and we've arranged to put up a stamp mill. The way the mines are booming, there's already more business than the mills in operation here can possibly handle, and there's bound to be plenty more. At any rate, that's how we figure. Our machinery's already on order; it's been promised for delivery at Bellport wharf, by river packet, sometime in early April.

'We're wondering if you'd like the consignment of hauling it from there?'

Dan Rawley stared. He looked at the others and then again at Owen. 'Do you realize what you're suggesting?' he demanded. 'I'm broke! I couldn't take on a contract of that size. I've got no wagons—no livestock . . .'

'We know all that,' Owen interrupted him. 'We also know this shipment is going to make us problems, whoever we ask to take the job.

144

Milling machinery is heavy, and it's big. Ordinary wagons won't serve. They have to be built to order, to our specifications. We'll expect to pay for that. We'd as soon pay you as anyone else.'

One of the others—a baldish, shrewd-mannered businessman named Ned McCabe—added, 'The rest of us are willing to take Frank's opinion, Rawley. He says you're as reliable a man as we can get. The fact you had a run of bad trouble, lately, doesn't need to alter anything.'

A little stunned, Dan pushed his fingers through his hair as a dozen different questions ran wild in his head. One thought narrowed his eyes then, made him point out, 'Up to now, Frank, you've always done business with Nate Archer. When I left him to go on my own, it wasn't with the idea of stealing any of his business.'

Owen's eye turned a trifle cold. He said firmly, 'Believe me! Whatever happens, Nate Archer gets no more of my business. I saw the condition of that last train that arrived for Work & Mantley—with that drunken Cap Shulte in charge!' Frank Owen shook his head. 'No—don't worry, Dan. You're not taking anything away from Archer. But you might as well have the business as anyone else. And there could be quite a lot more to follow.'

Dan Rawley took a long breath. With this consignment in his pocket, he knew Ross

Taggart could hardly refuse a bank loan to cover the cost of wagons and teams and personnel. Deliver this mill shipment successfully, and there seemed no limit to how far he and Hobie Drake could go from there.

It wasn't often, he thought, that a man who had just been wiped out could expect to have a whole new second chance dropped into his lap.

Owen, as though he thought Dan Rawley was hesitating, spoke again. 'There's one other thing. I don't want to seem to be appealing to your patriotism, but the fact remains this country's in trouble. I suppose you've been watching what's happened since the election. Things are falling apart, in a damned hurry. It looks like South Carolina's ready to vote secession, and if she does the rest of the slave states could follow.

'*I* don't know what's going to come of it, nor does anybody else. But if it should mean a war, the gold from these Denver mines is going to be awfully important, all of a sudden. By helping to make it available, we can be doing ourselves a favor, and helping our country, too.'

Dan Rawley held up a hand. 'You don't have to sell me the idea, Frank,' he said. He drew a breath. 'Thanks to all of you for your confidence. I'll grab the first stage East that I can get passage on, and I'll bring you your machinery. I'll do the best job I can.'

CHAPTER ELEVEN

A belated and uneasy springtime lay over the lands along the River. The winter, that had been slow in coming, turned out to be a stiff one and it hung on. But now, with the coming of April, life in the port towns began to quicken to the springing of new grass upon the Plains. A new season was getting underway.

Dan Rawley kept an anxious eye on the reports that came in as to the condition of the trail, as well as on those other stories from the East, where the dreaded specter of secession was now a fact. Inauguration Day had found the two halves of a disunited nation facing one another, under arms. Suddenly everyone's attention was riveted on the drama surrounding a beleaguered fortress in Charleston Harbor—an obscure place most people had never heard of. Every man seemed to know it all depended now on what would happen there, when Lincoln tried to send supplies to his garrison pinned down in Fort Sumter.

But Rawley's anxieties were nearer home than that. He and Hobie Drake, the latter barely able to get around at first with that knife cut only partly healed, had been working like demons from the time of Dan's return with the order from Frank Owen and his associates. Working to dimensions supplied by Owen, they had specially designed wagons ready—each twice the length of an ordinary freight rig—to haul the two boilers, and others reinforced against the weight of the heavy stamps and the other machinery. These, and the animals to pull them, were assembled now and being held on the prairie beyond the edge of town. But so far there was no sign of a river packet carrying the awaited mill.

Enforced idleness had a bad effect on Dan Rawley, turning him restless and moody. Even Vinnie Owen's company and her confidence in him weren't enough to help. He took to haunting the waterfront, listening to every word of river news and anxiously watching the Missouri. Each spring, after the first roiling melt of snow water off the plains, the river fell and stayed low until the release of water from the ice pack in the high mountains brought the so-called June rise. It was the worst time of year on the treacherous, snag-infested Big Muddy. Even the most experienced of pilots could have his trouble with shifting sandbars. Inside a single week there was word of two different sternwheelers having their hulls ripped out by sawyers, and being sent to the bottom.

It was enough to cause a man sleepless nights when he thought of Frank Owen and his associates, with more money than they could afford to lose tied up in this undelivered shipment. To say nothing of the note with his own signature that the bank was holding, in an amount that he didn't really like to think about . . .

He was sitting in a diner, having himself a lonely and moody midday meal, when a hand dropped upon his shoulder. It was Hobie Drake, and Dan quickly sensed his partner's excitement and hoped he knew the reason for it, even before Hobie spoke. 'Why ain't you at the wharf? The *Riverwind*'s just docked—didn't you hear her blow for landing? And from what the captain told me, looks like our stuff is in on her manifest!'

Dan left his plate of stew unfinished, threw down money to pay for it, and hurried out after his partner. He still couldn't imagine why he hadn't heard the boat whistle, unless he was too deep in funk for it to register. The one boat he'd been listening for, and he'd missed her!

There she was, tied up and unloading, her stacks scribbling smoke in twin pencil lines across the pale spring sky. They went aboard, dodging through the line of stevedores manhandling bales and boxes of freight down the gangplank. Minutes later they were staring at the piles of machinery lashed to the cargo deck.

'Godalmighty!' Hobie exclaimed huskily. 'Would you look at the size of that boiler! Dan, you reckon them rigs we built are gonna be big enough, after all?'

Dan Rawley nodded. 'They're big enough,' he said positively. 'Now it's for us to get loaded, and get on the road . . .'

*   *   *

Scowling bitterly, Wes Boyd watched the last of his chips raked in by the lean, prehensile fingers of the man across the table from him. He was dimly aware that the two other players in the game, with disgusted murmurs at the way the last hand had gone, were both pushing back their chairs, voicing their intentions to quit. For his own part, a wave of futile frustration at the unvarying run of his luck had him gripping his own hands tight, fighting the impulse to swear or smash something. The smoke-hazed air of Milligan's took on, for the moment, a reddish tinge which he knew was caused by the pound of the pulse behind his own eyes. When he had himself under control again, he carefully spread his hands and placed their wet palms upon the table top.

'I'm cleaned, for this evening,' he said hoarsely. 'Unless you want to take my paper.'

Vern Merrick, stacking chips, cocked an eyebrow at him. 'Don't you think I've taken quite a lot of your paper?' he murmured.

Boyd felt the warm color flood into his cheeks. Stung, he exclaimed angrily, 'You never objected!'

'Perhaps not. Still, maybe it's time we had a little talk about it.' He looked around. 'This is hardly the place though. As soon as I've finished here, let's take us a walk.'

The other managed a stern control over his tongue and his breathing as he waited and watched the gambler's neat, precise handling of the cards and the chips; but he felt as though the flesh had been pulled tight across his cheeks and that a weight had settled in his chest. This was a moment he had known was coming. He had been able somehow to keep from thinking too much about it.

Minutes later they were walking in no great haste along the sidewalks of the town, breathing the freshness of the spring night and the raw, dark smells that came from the river bottom. Merrick had fired up a cigar and he seemed content to enjoy it in silence. Boyd checked the tumult of angry, half-formed speech, knowing instinctively that this other man had him in a bad spot and that it was best to hold back and let him show what he meant to do about it. Only once, after minutes had passed in his way without a word being spoken, did he demand harshly, 'Where do you think you're taking me, for this talk you wanted?'

'We've just arrived,' Merrick answered blandly, and turned in at a gateway in a high, plank wall.

Recognizing Nate Archer's down-at-heels freight yard, Wes Boyd balked. 'Why here?' he

151

demanded suspiciously. But Merrick was already crossing the yard, toward the flat-roofed office building where lamplight showed at the windows; and the other had little choice but to follow. Scowling blackly, he let the gambler usher him up the three steps and through the door. As they entered, Nate Archer looked up from his desk at the far end of the room; the dome of his bald head gleamed under the ceiling lamp.

In a barrel chair at the edge of the shadows, big Cap Shulte sat like a lump with elbows on the arms of his barrel chair and big hands dangling limply. He eyed the newcomers with wolfish interest.

Not waiting for a greeting from either of these, Vern Merrick said in a pleasant tone, 'Here's our friend Boyd. I brought him, like we agreed, so we could discuss our little problem.'

Wes Boyd's head jerked toward the gambler. 'Now, see here! I've got nothing to do with either of these men.'

'That's where you're mistaken,' Merrick answered. And now, leaning forward in his chair, Nate Archer opened a drawer of the desk and removed an envelope, from which he took a familiar-looking sheaf of papers. He fanned them with his thumb and tapped the edges of the papers on the desk top, to square them.

Boyd was staring. 'Where did he get those?' he demanded hoarsely.

'From me,' Merrick told him. 'I never told you, but Nate Archer has been bankrolling my game. So, you see, anything you owe to me—you owe both of us.'

Archer tapped the papers with the back of a hand. His black eyes probed Boyd's. 'I didn't realize we were carrying you for such a large amount. Of course,' and the freighter's lips quirked in an icy smile, 'I suppose you're good for it?'

'Of course!' Boyd snapped, trying to keep any trace of panic from his voice.

The barrel chair creaked as big Cap Shulte shifted his weight. 'If he's thinking of welshing, I can damn well make him wish he hadn't!'

Boyd looked at the big hands, and at the grin that showed the Dutchman's teeth. He tried to speak and couldn't. It was Merrick, the gambler, who said quickly, 'Oh, that ain't going to be necessary. His uncle's good for it, even if he ain't.'

'I'll take care of this!' Wes Boyd said quickly—too quickly. 'You don't have to drag Frank Owen into it.'

Nate Archer's eyes narrowed thoughtfully. 'You act like that's the last thing in the world you want to see happen. It wouldn't be that it's Owen's money you been playing with?' He read his answer in the younger man's look; he wagged his bald head. 'Now, that just wasn't a very smart thing to do! At least, it wasn't very smart to lose!'

153

A nerve had begun leaping in the muscle of Wes Boyd's jaw. He looked at these three—at Cap Shulte, who was the physical menace; at Nate Archer, whom he'd always dismissed contemptuously as a failed businessman but who, he saw now, had a vein of iron in him that came to the fore when he held the advantage as he did now. And he looked at Vern Merrick, the author of his undoing—and suddenly he remembered a night, months ago, when that yellow-haired tough, Hobie Drake, had pushed his way to a poker table at Milligan's and had tried to warn him that he was letting himself be made the victim of a cheat. All at once he found himself wishing he could have paid more attention.

He ran a hand across his bearded cheeks and said, in a voice he tried to hold steady and self-assured, 'There's no call to make threats. Give me a little time and you'll have your money.'

The freighter's whole face went through a series of grimaces, as though what Boyd had said caused him a pained and embarrassing reaction. But when he spoke his voice sounded smug. 'I ain't a rich man, like your uncle—it ain't so easy for me to wait for what's owed me.' He wagged his bald head. 'I think you better have a chair, Mr. Boyd.'

There was an empty one, waiting for him, across the desk from Archer. As Boyd reluctantly lowered himself onto it, laying his hat on his knee, the freighter picked up the sheaf of notes and riffled through them idly. The thought struck Boyd that this whole scene had been carefully staged and prepared for him. Anger mingling with the hopelessness of his position, he drew a breath. 'All right,' he said. 'Let's have it straight. What have you decided you want from me?'

Archer looked at the gambler, who had leaned his shoulders against the wall. He looked at Boyd, and nodded. 'That's much better; now we can really talk. Who knows—it might even to be possible to tear up these notes and forget they ever existed.'

'I'm listening,' Boyd said shortly.

Nate Archer drummed his fingers on the desk top. 'I understand,' he said, 'Dan Rawley left for Denver a few days ago, with a special shipment for your uncle—business that should by rights have been mine, if Rawley hadn't stolen it from me.'

Boyd nodded. 'It was a quartz mill. Two boilers and several tons of machinery.'

'I've just had word from some people out in that country, friends of mine—or of Vern Merrick's, actually,' the freighter added, correcting himself. 'It seems they're in the market for just such an outfit as that.'

'Let them order one.'

'Takes too long. They can't afford the delay.'

Merrick shifted position, the shoulders of

his box coat whispering against the wall as he moved. 'I don't think you understand, Boyd,' he cut in. 'These friends of mine are pretty anxious. A situation has arisen. Meanwhile they've got the money to pay for what they want—and they'll pay well.'

Wes Boyd was studying the gambler—the narrow face, the bad complexion, the pouches under the deep-set eyes. He said suddenly, 'You and I have never really talked politics; still, I've wondered a time or two if you might not have Southern leanings. These friends of yours: It wouldn't happen they represent Secessionist interests, by any chance?'

The face turned subtly dangerous, the cold eyes narrowed. 'That bothers you?'

'Not a bit,' Wes Boyd answered with a shrug. 'I'm merely curious.'

'Let's tell him the rest of it, then,' Nate Archer urged the gambler. He himself proceeded to do so. 'As you've guessed, these men are Southern mine owners, and loyal. If there should be war, they're going to want to send their gold South to help the Confederacy. But the mills where their mineral must be processed are all in Northern hands, and of course shipping crude ore is out of the question. The only answer is for them somehow to set up milling equipment of their own.'

Boyd was staring. He said slowly, 'I begin to see it. I think you have some idea of getting

156

ahold of the shipment Rawley is taking West with him!'

'I take it you don't approve?' Archer said, after a moment.

'How could I? I don't give a damn about Rawley; but my uncle has a small fortune invested in that mill. Losing it could ruin him.'

The freighter lifted a shoulder. He said, 'I imagine Frank Owen can always manage to take care of himself.'

Merrick put in, his voice gently mocking, 'I'm sure he'd be touched to know how concerned you are, friend Boyd. But maybe not so much if he saw these notes!'

That silenced Boyd, sent him deeper into his chair, his shoulders slumping. After a moment he said sullenly, 'I don't think you can get away with it, anyhow. Rawley and that Drake will put up a fight.'

'That's where Cap comes in.'

Archer waggled a thumb at the big Dutchman, who grinned showing all his teeth. 'My boys and me, we'll take the fight out of 'em. Damned quick!'

Wes Boyd ran a hand across his bearded cheeks. He said, 'Nobody's told me yet where *I* come in.'

'That's true.' Nate Archer built his fingers into a steeple, looked at the other man across their tips, his bald head tilted on one side. 'You hold Owen's power of attorney, don't you?'

Boyd nodded warily.

'Then you're able to act for him, disposing of property belonging either to him or his partners. The people I speak of will pay a good bonus for legal title. So, we want you along for supercargo—to sign the papers.'

'But—I could never show my face in this town again!'

'You've been telling me all winter,' Merrick reminded him, 'the only thing you ever wanted out of this town was *out*—if you only had a stake. So, here's your chance, if you mean it. It's the biggest melon you'll likely ever see a slice of!'

Nate Archer said, 'Well? What about it?'

Boyd looked around at the waiting faces, in a stillness in which he could almost hear the tick of the watch in his own waistcoat pocket. Scowling, he thrust out a hand. 'Give me the notes.'

'Not quite yet.' Archer picked them up, stowed them away in his pocket. 'You get them later—as part of your cut. For the time being, they'll act as a sort of guarantee of good faith.'

Wes Boyd slowly lowered the hand, and drew a breath. That was how it was, then. He had no real choice. He said heavily, 'When do we leave?'

He saw how the careful tension of the room eased, how the three of them visibly relaxed. 'At once,' Nate Archer answered him. 'First thing tomorrow. Cap's boys are all ready to

158

ride. Rawley's got almost a week's start on us, but traveling light we should have no trouble overtaking him.

'We'll have a drink on this,' he added pleasantly, and pulling open a desk drawer brought out a half-full bottle with which to seal the agreement.

CHAPTER TWELVE

Vinnie Owen had spent the morning seated at her desk, writing letters—using it as a way to keep her mind occupied, though in her present mood she found it a worrisome chore. Perhaps, she thought, it was the uncertain temper of the day that oppressed her—the spatters of rain flung against her window, the restless shuttling of sunlight and cloud shadow flowing across the walls of her room.

She missed her father, and she couldn't help but think of Dan Rawley somewhere on the westward trail. Besides, there was now the vaguely troubling matter of her cousin Wes, who had left that morning on some unexplained business. Brushing aside any questions of hers, he had simply packed and left abruptly. At the store, no one could tell her anything. What made it all the worse, he had apparently gone without even making arrangements for managing the business in his

159

absence.

Vinnie had led a sheltered life, and knew almost nothing of the family's business interests. She felt ignorant and helpless in this emergency. She reached for a fresh sheet of notepaper, to begin a letter to her father— dismally aware, even as she wrote the date at the head of the paper, how much time must pass before he could receive it or she could hope to get an answer.

There was a tap at her door. 'Miz Vinnie?' Sarah, now the only other person beside herself in this big and lonely house, put her head inside. 'There's a white gentleman downstairs, says he want to see you.'

The girl frowned. 'He didn't tell you his name?'

'No ma'am.' Sarah appeared sourly disapproving. 'He's a most peculiar lookin' gentleman. He says he's got news for you— something about your cousin Wes. And Mister Rawley.'

She could not have explained her feeling that this caller, whoever he was, had brought her news of terrible importance. With purely feminine instinct, she glanced into a mirror, almost unconsciously touched a hand to her hair. Then, steeling herself against whatever she was about to learn, she went down through the silent house to find an ancient, bright-eyed stranger standing in the hallway, his hat in both twisted hands.

He was bent and twisted by time, and so frail in appearance that Vinnie was instantly moved to invite him into the parlor and to a seat. But the old fellow refused. 'Don't want to track mud on your carpet. I'll just say my piece and go. You wouldn't know nothing about me, ma'am; I'm just old Charlie—Charlie Clewes.'

'Of course!' she said quickly. 'You work for Mr. Archer. Dan Rawley has told me about you.'

'Why, has he now?' The old man seemed highly pleased to know someone had mentioned him. He grinned and bobbed his head that he held at what looked as though it must be a painful angle.

'Sarah tells me you have news . . .'

'I'm willing to bet it's news!' the old man said grimly. 'At least, I'll wager that fellow Boyd never gave out word where he was goin' this morning, in such an all-fired hurry!'

She admitted it. 'He didn't say anything at all. But—how did *you* know he was gone?'

'My boss went with him, that's how! Along with a gambler named Merrick, and that fellow Cap Shulte and a half dozen of Shulte's tough friends.'

Vinnie knew that last name; she stared at Charlie Clewes in disbelief. 'I just don't understand! What possible business could my cousin Wes be having with people like Shulte, or Nate Archer for that matter? Why would he have to go anywhere with them—on hardly any notice?'

'Well, nobody *told* me,' the old man admitted. 'I'm just old Charlie, y' understand—somebody underfoot, that don't matter. But I got ears, and I done heard enough to set me wondering. And happens there's one of Shulte's tough crowd that I knew wouldn't be leaving with 'em because he's got his arm broke in a fight. So, soon as the rest pulled out I went around to where this feller Conlon is staying, and I tuck along a bottle to help get him oiled up before I started asking questions. I wormed out of him what I hadn't been able to guess.'

And standing there on her doorsill, shifting worn-out boots and turning his battered hat between gnarled and broken hands, Charlie told the girl a story that drained the color from her cheeks and made her put a hand against the wall, actually afraid for a moment that she might do the fashionable, ladylike thing and faint.

She found her voice; her mouth was dry and speech came with difficulty. 'You suppose this is really true? Why, it could *ruin* my father. And—Dan Rawley!'

'Reckon there's not much doubt what they got planned for *that* young feller,' Charlie Clewes muttered darkly, 'if they can take him by surprise—especially if Cap Shulte has his way. The Dutchman's been wanting nothing but to kill him for a lot of months now!'

Vinnie passed the back of a trembling hand across her face, appalled and numbed by the run of her thoughts. 'But there must be *some* way—something that can be done . . .'

Charlie Clewes shook his head. 'If I'd thought so, I'd be talkin' to George Byam or somebody. Hell, lady—they've *gone*! And ain't no law, or no nothin', can reach out into the wilderness and stop them now!'

The truth of what he said was so obvious that she found herself nodding, absently and despairingly. 'I know, I know!' But then, she paused, confronted by a thought so stunning in its audacity that she had to back off for a second look at it. Even as she was telling herself, No—it's out of the question! she knew that, with so very much at stake, even this faint hope must be grabbed at.

'Mr. Clewes!' Her voice held a sudden fierce intensity that made him blink. 'Our horse and carriage are out in the shed. Could you hitch them for me? And do you think you can handle the reins?'

'What!' He gasped at her. 'Whoa, now! You ain't thinking of going *after* 'em? A beat-up old man and a girl, in a buggy? Why, they's no *sense* to it! And anyway, Archer and them has got hours on us—and they'll be travelin' fast. We'd never hope to catch them.'

Her hand went out and seized his arm, stringy and tough within the worn coat sleeve. 'I'm not asking for you to go after them,' she assured him quickly. 'I just want you to take me down river—to Leavenworth. I can get the Denver coach from there. Now, move— please!—while I get packed.' He was still gaping blankly when Vinnie opened the big door and all but shoved him through it.

Closing the door, Vinnie turned toward the staircase to discover the broad figure of Sarah blocking her way. The woman showed an expression of utter shock. 'Miz Vinnie!' she cried, aghast. 'You lost your *mind*? You don't need to think I'm going to let you do any such foolish thing as this!'

Vinnie's jaw set, her eye glinted—but it was less from determination than from the fear that she would panic and give way. 'Sarah, don't you see I *have* to go? I can't stand by and not even make an effort to warn Pa what's happening.'

'But to travel all that way—alone!'

'I won't be alone. There'll be a whole coachload of people.'

'You know what I mean!' Sarah snapped. 'Besides, you can just as easy tell your pa all he needs to know in a letter. It'd get to him just as quick.'

She protested, 'While I sit here, and wait, and go crazy?' She shook her head firmly. 'There's no use talking to me, Sarah!' And she moved past and started running up the stairs to her room. Behind her sounded a massive martyr's sigh.

'I'll get out my old carpetbag, then. ' 'Cause, I'm goin' with you.'

'Oh, no, you're not!' Vinnie whirled, halfway up the steps. 'It's going to be hard enough for one person to find a place on that stagecoach. You stay here!'

She left the outraged woman sputtering, and refused to wait for further argument. She could only imagine what Sarah's reaction would have been if she knew what Vinnie really had in her mind.

*   *   *

The Leavenworth agent for the Overland Stage Company didn't seem to know what to make of the pale and desperate-looking girl in the gray traveling dress who had appeared at his window. He looked past her, hunting for some sign of a male escort. Finding none, he scowled at her again through the thick lenses of his spectacles. 'Denver, miss?' he repeated. 'I just don't really know about that . . .'

'I have the fare,' she said quickly and, fumbling in her reticule, brought out a wadded handful of greenbacks. 'So don't you have to sell me a ticket?'

'I'll sell you the ticket,' he answered stiffly. 'But do you think it's exactly the trip for a young lady to be making alone? You *are* alone, aren't you?'

'I can take care of myself.'

'I wonder if you know exactly what you're getting into. That coach carries as many fares as we can crowd aboard. It's seven days to Denver—and once she starts rolling, she don't stop except for meals and a change of horses ...'

'Please!' the girl exclaimed, with a look of anguish that melted him. 'My pa's there. I *have* to reach him!'

Wavering, he said, 'What about luggage?'

'This is all.' She picked up the carpetbag from the floor at her feet.

The agent gave in. 'All right,' he said, and he took her money and made out the ticket. As he handed it to her, he pointed with his chin. 'There's a bench right outside. Coach will be making up in half an hour. You set there, and I'll see that you get on it.'

'Thank you!' Vinnie Owen exclaimed. 'Thank you so much!' The grateful smile she gave him captured him completely.

She went to tell the reluctant and troubled Charlie Clewes that everything was arranged, and to send him starting home over the river road to Bellport. Afterward she found the bench the agent had spoken of and, with carpetbag at her feet and reticule in her lap, obediently took up her vigil.

It appeared to last a great deal longer than half an hour. As she waited, a crowd began to accumulate, a few at a time at first, then a steady flux of people who filled the station and

166

the sidewalk and the area of the cloud-dappled street in front of it. They were nearly all men—milling about and smoking and spitting and creating an ever greater volume of rough male talk. Vinnie watched in dismay. She was certain it would be impossible for this many to find places on the coach, and yet it was apparently what they all had in mind.

Suddenly from the telegraph office two doors below the station, a man wearing sleeve protectors and a green eyeshade came bursting out brandishing a sheet of paper. He had to shout his news twice before he could make himself heard but, when he did, every other matter was instantly forgotten. Vinnie had caught only a sentence or two: 'Fort Sumter . . . The shelling began early this morning . . . They're still at it!' It was enough to bring her to her feet. Sickened, engulfed with horror, she placed a hand against the wall for support and stood there in a daze while all of Leavenworth seemed to go crazy around her.

Men were shouting and cursing, in a frenzy of excitement. Horsemen went racing insanely up the street and back again, firing off handguns, yelling the news of war. Yonder, in front of a saloon, an argument started and instantly became a fight that swelled to a melee, as new recruits came running to throw themselves into it with shouts and swinging fists. And now, at the very height of all this hubbub and confusion, the big stagecoach, with its six-horse hitch, came rolling out from behind the station and rocked to a stand for loading.

Vinnie, eyeing the clumsy, weathered vehicle, took a moment to remember that it actually had some connection with her. When the agent, himself excited enough, tossed a bulky mail sack up to the driver's boot and then came and spoke to her, she looked back at him like someone in a stupor. He had to repeat himself: 'Come along, miss. If you'll take a rear seat, by the window, you'll find that's the most comfortable for you.' She managed a nod to show she understood, and let him take her carpetbag and lead her over to the coach.

She had never before been inside one of these big Western stages. It was a tremendous climb up the single metal step, and the body of the coach swayed on its leather thorough braces as she fumbled her way to the seat. It had padding of a kind, but when she settled into her place by the window she knew already that this was going to be an ordeal.

The coach began to load A portly middle-aged man settled himself ponderously beside her, and next to him a woman carrying a baby—Vinnie wondered if she actually meant to hold that baby on her lap all the way to Denver! The rest of the travelers were men. A dropseat was let down across the middle of the coach, and six more passengers filled the

168

remaining spaces—nine people, crammed into a space that left no one any room for moving, the knees of the man who sat facing Vinnie all but touching her own. And now the coach swayed and bucked as others rushed to clamber up the sides and find places on the roof. On every hand rose a babbling of heated debate about the news from Charleston Harbor.

Even though the windows were open, in this press of bodies Vinnie felt stifled. She thought, If they could only get started! Yet even now, with the coach loaded and the rear boot shield strapped down and the horses stomping and restless in the harness, they continued to wait during long, dragging minutes. Presently, a guard came from the station carrying a rifle, and climbed to the forward boot. Then at last the driver himself appeared—a man in stag pants and polished boots, with buckskin fringes on his gauntlets and a whip coiled over one arm. He took his time checking the harness, afterward swinging with practiced ease up the high front wheel. A horse handler passed the six leathers up to him.

A sudden whoop and crack of the whip, and the teams leaned into their collars. The passengers were unprepared and took a neck-popping lurch; the baby woke, screaming. And to the slam and bang of timbers and a boiling of dust, the streets of Leavenworth blurred by and they were launched into the immensity of the plains beyond.

It did not take Vinnie long to discover what this would be like. Despite the thorough braces, enough of the jostling of the wheels over rough road was transmitted through the thin seat padding. If it weren't for being jammed into the corner by the portly bulk of her neighbor, she supposed things could have been even worse. In a very short while she felt numbed and bruised from the waist down. And as she clung to the window frame, she wondered how the passengers up top managed to hold their places at all.

She listened numbly to the voices of the men crammed with her in this noisy discomfort. The baby whimpered, slept, woke and cried again. A fog of dust hung everywhere in suspension, and if she wanted to breathe she breathed it, laced with the smoke from a half dozen cigars and pipes. The man facing her leaned to the open window from time to time to loose a gobbet of brown tobacco juice into the wind. Vinnie cringed away every time she saw him do it.

An hour passed—another. They rode in silence now. After a while, even the excitement over Fort Sumter had to yield to a speechless effort of sheer endurance. The empty land swept by, under a restless shuttling of sunlight and cloud shadow. The hills on the horizon showed fresh with a new green of springtime; nearer, everything was a uniform earth-color, of brown mud churned up by countless turning wheels. Now and then they passed freight and emigrant wagons, stretched out in line of march or encamped back from the trail. Teamsters and mounted horsemen lifted hands in greeting as the coach rocked by.

They rolled up to a station—a mere hovel of cottonwood logs and mud under a sod roof, with a barn and corral behind it and a dugout well with a sweep. Fresh teams were ready to be hooked into place; within minutes they were tearing on again. Ahead the sun was dropping, filling the whole western sky with a brassy glare that stabbed at Vinnie so that she ducked her head, and tried to shield her eyes with her fingers.

She roused with a start to realize that she must, incredibly enough, have dozed off. The sun was gone, the swift prairie twilight settling under a canopy of stars. The coach had halted before another of the low roofed prairie soddies, whose windows made yellow squares of lamplight against the dusk. People were stirring and now the door was jerked open. The driver told them: 'Home station. You can get a meal inside. We'll be here forty minutes.'

Vinnie was the last to climb out of the coach. She had to place a hand on the rear wheel a moment to steady herself. Her body was stiff and pounded sore, and she had a headache; but the cool wind that breathed across the distances felt refreshing against her cheeks. She tried to push some shape into the wreckage of her hair, and brush a few wrinkles from her traveling dress. Afterwards she followed the rest into the station.

It was crude enough, with a tamped dirt floor, a plank bar across one end of the main room, a single homemade table with benches running along either side. The other passengers were already seated, serving themselves from bowls and platters steaming on the table. The food neither looked nor smelled very appetizing.

She discovered she was the only woman in the room—the one with the baby, she thought, must have gone somewhere alone to nurse it. The stage driver was standing at the bar, discussing Sumter with a man with weather-coarsened features, dressed in shapeless homespuns. Judging him to be the proprietor, on an impulse she approached this man and said falteringly, 'Please—I'm anxious to know if you've seen anything of some people who might have been through here. They left Bellport five days ago . . .'

'For Denver?' the man broke in. At her nod, he said, 'But they wouldn't of come this way, lady. That Bellport trail don't feed into the Overland for some distance north and west of here. You better ask somewhere further along the line.'

'I see. Thank you,' she said. It had been a foolish question. She should have realized before she asked it.

The driver said, 'You'd best eat if you intend to. Stage don't wait for nobody.'

The food was miserable—stew concocted of stringy meat and mushy vegetables; salt-rising biscuits like rocks, and coffee black enough to float them. If it was this bad at the first station on the line, Vinnie preferred not to think what she was likely to find waiting for her farther from civilization. By the time she was finished, the order to load the coach was being given.

Full dark had come; the side lamps had been lit. Fresh horses were already in place and the deck passengers were scrambling for places of vantage up top. Her portly seat companion helped Vinnie aboard and sagged down beside her with a groan, announcing that he was certain he would never survive six days and nights of this torture.

To the driver's yell, and the gun-like pop of his whip—Vinnie wondered how he could possibly manage, both hands being filled already with the reins of half a dozen stage horses—they were on their way again.

Night deepened, broken by the circle of flickering light from the coach lamps, and the occasional glow of a freighter's camp. As the wind turned chilly, the leather side curtains were rolled down and fastened, closing the passengers into the intimacy of a cramped and swaying room whose only illumination was the glow of a cigar or pipe against a mouth or jaw.

Vinnie's neighbor tried to make conversation. She gathered that he was a businessman with some sort of mission at Denver. The woman with the baby, it seemed, was an officer's wife en route to join her husband at Fort Kearney. Vinnie offered little information about herself.

She was determined to get some sleep somehow, and toward midnight—thanks to sheer exhaustion—she must have managed, for she woke to find the coach halted, and to hear an exchange of talk in the night outside. One of the passengers said they had come to a ferry. Pulling back the edge of the leather curtain, Vinnie had a glimpse of a lighted window, of dark tree heads blotting out the stars. The big coach and its teams were maneuvered down the bank and onto the bobbing raft. She could see the gleam and soft shine of the water. It offered a welcome break, for these few quiet minutes of the crossing. But after that they were crawling up the farther bank and, with a final halloo from the ferryman, the horses were put into the collars again.

The next thing Vinnie Owen knew, her eyes opened onto a gray hint of dawn that seemed to filter a grainy light into the darkness of the coach, showing her the faces of her fellow travelers as though carved from stone—dull-eyed, expressionless, stolidly enduring.

CHAPTER THIRTEEN

The near front wheel struck what must have been a tremendous chuck hole and hit bottom with a grinding crash that hurled everyone against his neighbor. The coach tipped ponderously, slewed half around and settled in a chorus of excited yells from within and up top. The driver must have halted his teams in time, with rare speed of reflex. Horses squealed, dust slowly settled.

Someone pawed at a door handle, forced it open and tumbled outside while the deck passengers scrambled down from their perch. Vinnie, half crushed under the lurching weight of the big man next to her, could only grit her teeth and endure it as he managed to remove himself, fighting the steep and unnatural pitch of the coach floor.

Men were milling around outside. Coach horses stomped and jingled their harness. Now the downslope door was wrenched open and a confused babble of voices broke off as the driver said, in savage temper, 'All right, you can get out, damn it! We've busted a thorough brace!'

Vinnie was the last to be helped, dazed and weak-kneed, out of the crazily tilted coach. Someone demanded bitterly, 'What happens to us now?'

'Take your pick,' the driver told him with short patience. 'Rock Creek Station is just past that next dip. I'll cripple in with the coach and try to get it fixed, you can either wait till I send back a rig to haul you in, or you can hoof it.'

He turned back to the swearing, and gave his attention again to his problems. One of the leather braces was plainly broken, and this stagecoach would not be running again until it could be replaced. From the driver's manner, it looked to be a major operation.

Vinnie Owen had already decided she was glad of the opportunity to get a little exercise. A straggle of passengers who had accepted the inevitable were starting off along the road on foot. Having set her hair and clothing to rights as best she could without a mirror, she struck out after them, swinging her reticule.

She must not have looked too bad despite her rumpled appearance, for one of the men gave her a glance and lagged a step, waiting for her. Vinnie walked straight on without so much as a look, swiftly side-stepping when she thought he meant to grab her arm. She only hoped she hadn't let him see the fright that must have been in her face. After all, she tried to tell herself that it was foolish to be so timid. These people were all in the same boat as herself. Surely she was safe enough, in plain daylight.

It was good to have firm ground under her, to step out and stretch cramped muscles even though her shoes were not the best for walking. The morning was clear, with a few clouds standing about in the pale high sky, and a wind from the west that smelled fresh and pleasant after the interior of the coach. She was almost able to forget, for that moment, the anxious concerns pressing on her. She drew aside out of the way as the big, mud-stained coach rolled slowly past her, held to a crawl by the damaged thorough brace. Then the road dipped ahead of her and she could see the buildings and pole corral of the station, with a bridge spanning the timbered stream beyond. The rolling hills of Nebraska seemed to form a wide and shallow cup here, all around the wider rim of the horizon.

When Vinnie Owen reached the station, the teams were being unhooked from the crippled stage and led away to the corral by a stable-hand, and a knot of passengers and station personnel were gathered about to discuss what needed to be done. From the tone of their voices she gathered, in dismay, that repairs might take some time.

Over at the door of the main house, a woman appeared for a moment to shade her eyes with her forearm, watching the scene in the yard, then after a moment went back inside. Vinnie had started in that direction, when she noticed a man who stood a little apart with hands shoved in the pockets of his unbuttoned coat—seemingly, the only one

177

untroubled by the accident. As she approached, cold black eyes regarded her. In a decided Carolina accent he asked, 'Ma'am, can I help you?'

'You're connected with the station?'

'I built it.' He was swarthy, not unhandsome, with a sweeping dark mustache and trimmed whiskers, and hair that reached almost to his collar—Vinnie had a feeling he thought rather well of himself. He touched his hat brim, his eyes bold on her face. 'The name's Dave McCanles.'

She told her story: 'I'm very much concerned to learn about a freighting outfit that must have come through here in the last few days. I wonder if you could tell me anything about it . . .' She faltered, as she saw the interest in his eyes congeal; suddenly her cheeks heated up as she sensed his opinion of a woman who would chase across country after a wagon freight outfit. But she stood her ground. 'It's really important that I try to catch up with them. Something that's come up, since they started.'

McCanles lifted a shoulder. 'I wouldn't know anything about it. Since I sold out to the stage line, I don't come around here very often—I got a ranch over on the Blue to keep me busy. You better talk to Wellman, here. He runs the place now.'

A narrow-faced, harassed-looking man had left the group around the crippled stagecoach

178

and was walking rapidly toward the station, scowling at his own thoughts. McCanles called to him, beckoning with the crook of a finger. Wellman halted, looking from McCanles to the girl with distracted impatience, as the big man explained Vinnie's problem.

'I don't remember every freight outfit that crosses the toll bridge,' he said gruffly, shaking his head. Nor did the name of Dan Rawley seem to register with him. 'This is only my first season. Isn't there anything else you can tell me?'

She tried as best she could. 'There were a dozen wagons—big ones, filled with milling machinery. And two huge boilers—'

'Why didn't you say that before! Yeah, there was such an outfit went through late yesterday. I'd say it must have been the one you're looking for.'

'Yesterday!' she exclaimed. 'They couldn't be too far ahead, then!'

'No more that six, eight miles, the rate those bull trains travel.' But he shook his head as he saw her sudden eagerness. 'I don't know about you catching up with them, though—not in that busted stagecoach. We're going to have a real job, rigging up a new thorough brace.'

Her hopes sagged. Desperately she suggested, 'Could you rent me a horse?'

'Lady, I got no saddle stock here—only the animals belonging to the company.'

McCanles spoke up. 'You got a wagon,

179

Horace. Maybe somebody wouldn't mind hitching up and driving her down the trail a piece.'

'I'll be glad to pay them for their trouble,' Vinnie put in quickly.

'Sounds like a job for that Duck Bill fellow,' said McCanles, when Wellman hesitated. 'Let him make himself useful around here, for once.'

He indicated the stocktender, just now returning from putting the stage teams into the big pole corral that stood between barn and creek. Horace Wellman, distracted with larger problems, pulled off his hat and shoved stubby fingers through his hair. 'Why, it'd be all right with me, I guess, if he's agreeable.' He raised his voice in a shout. 'Over here, Jim.'

The man heard and veered in their direction. He looked to Vinnie, as he approached, a nondescript young fellow, tall and thin, dressed in jeans and hickory shirt. 'What now?' he demanded, in a surly voice.

Wellman told him, 'First, I want you to drive the wagon out and pick up a pile of luggage they unloaded from the stage. I understand, too, there's a woman and a baby—maybe some other passengers who didn't feel like hoofing it.'

The young fellow seemed to take his orders as a personal affront. He lifted his shoulders and started to slouch away again, but Wellman called him back. 'When you get that done, Jim, the young lady here is interested in a quartz mill outfit that pulled through here yesterday afternoon. Likely won't be any great problem, catching up with them. I told her you'd be willing to haul her.'

'I'll pay whatever your time is worth to you,' Vinnie said again.

McCanles, listening, gave a snort of heavy derision. 'There *ain't* that much money! Lady, you better pay Wellman—at least it would help cover some of the grub he puts away.'

Baited, the young fellow swung to stare hotly at McCanles. He was rather odd-looking, Vinnie noticed: beardless, with steel-blue eyes—flashing now with anger—and a strange, protruding upper lip that gave a peculiar cast to his whole profile. Before he could make hot answer, Horace Wellman gave him an elbow in the ribs and that turned him aside. 'Get going, Jim. I reckon nobody's going to ask the lady to pay. We're only glad to help.'

*   *   *

The wagon was a cumbersome vehicle but, with a spirited team of stage horses in the harness, the young man with the reins managed to get fair speed out of it. Vinnie clung to her place, clutching her reticule and trying not to get bounced off the springless seat while, in the wagonbed behind them, her carpetbag slid around and thumped the boards

181

as they hit the low places. Her companion said little of anything, scarcely took his brooding stare off the rumps of his horses when she tried to make conversation. She found this scarcely flattering, but she decided her companion was a very strange person, and he seemed to be in short temper. She had an idea, somehow, that he was brooding over his treatment by the bearded man at Rock Creek Station. It seemed to be an old grievance.

To make conversation, she asked, 'You heard about the news from Sumter? Isn't it terrible! I suppose there's no chance but that it's going to be war ...'

He nodded curtly but said nothing, his brooding stare set straight ahead. A gust of wind seized Vinnie's hat and tried to pull it free of its pins. She clamped a hand to it. After a while she tried again: 'Did you happen to see those wagons when they came through yesterday?'

His head tilted, a bare couple of inches. 'Yep.'

'I wonder if, by any chance, you'd also remember some horsemen who might have ridden by sometime since. They'd be a large group—ten or twelve perhaps, traveling together?'

He thought about this. 'Never saw them,' he decided, and Vinnie began to know a hope that, for all their headstart and the shorter route they'd taken, the stage might even so have passed Wes and Shulte and the rest somewhere on the road.

But her companion quickly dampened these hopes. 'It don't mean too much. They needn't necessarily have come past the station. Plenty of other crossings a horseman could take—and no toll to pay.' Still, she decided she must cling, as long as possible, to any encouraging thought. She needed it.

The sun swung overhead, straight up in the pale sky. They sighted a wagon outfit in noon camp, off the trail, and Vinnie watched it hopefully but decided it wasn't the one she thought. It fell behind and they were alone again with the steady slogging of the horses, the rattle and bang of wagon timbers.

Something had made her curious. 'I thought Mister Wellman said your name was Jim,' she observed. 'But I heard that other man call you—' The words 'Duck Bill' died in her throat, for she glanced at his profile just then and noticed again the protruding upper lip, and thought perhaps she understood. Hastily, she substituted other words: '—I thought he called you something else.'

She saw his mouth harden. 'My name,' he said sharply, 'is James Butler Hickok. And if that loud mouth McCanles don't quit riding me every time he comes around the station, I just might give him cause to remember it!'

He looked at Vinnie as he said it, and she would always afterward wonder at the bitter ferocity in his steel-blue stare, that made her shudder a little in spite of herself.

As it turned out, they very nearly missed their goal. The wagons had made noon camp, half hidden in creek-bank willows some distance off the trail. It was Vinnie who sighted them and, pointing, said quickly, 'Doesn't that look like them, Mister Hickok?' He looked, grunted 'I reckon,' and swung his team wide.

Vinnie searched anxiously as they neared. Above the canvas wagontops, smoke spiraled from a cookfire; yonder, draft cattle were grazing, still under the yoke. But she made out no human figures at all and her keen impatience mounted. Then, partially hidden by a couple of other wagons, she caught sight of a big boiler lashed to two running gears that had been stripped of their bodies and put together tandem fashion. And at once her heart beat high, as she knew she had actually overtaken the train she had been hunting for so desperately.

Hickok was just tooling his wagon to a halt when a pair of men stepped into view around the tailgate of big, specially-built rigs filled with milling machinery, a giant flywheel riding the top of its load. Horror shocked through Vmnie as one of the men lifted his head, and beneath the flat, wide brim of his hat she recognized her cousin Wes. Gone cold to the fingertips, she could only sit helpless as he

184

circled the team horses, coming around to her side of the wagon.

The second man, she saw now, was Nate Archer—his unaccustomed hours in saddle, under the strong prairie sun, had given the freighter a rather violent sunburn. There was a gun belt and holster strapped to his leg, and beneath the open front of Wes Boyd's canvas jacket Vinnie could see the handle of a weapon shoved behind his waistband.

Wes put a hand on the rim of the wheel and smiled at Vinnie, but behind the smile his eyes were furious. 'Well—my dear cousin Lavinia!' he exclaimed. 'A real surprise!'

She found her voice. Her hands were clenched so tightly that they ached. 'Yes,' she said faintly. 'I—I know.'

'Whatever are you doing here?' He eyed the wagon. 'On this!'

'The stagecoach broke down at Rock Creek Station,' she answered, miserably. 'Mr. Hickok was good enough to bring me on from there . . .'

'Kind of him,' her cousin said, his voice mocking her, his cold eye sliding on to study the young fellow holding the reins. 'We'll have to reward him, won't we?'

Vinnie saw Nate Archer, on the far side of the wagon, scowling and rubbing his palm on the handle of that holstered gun. Hickok, she knew, was unarmed. Suddenly, the thought that she might have been the means of bringing an outsider into mortal danger shook her. Almost stammering, she said, 'He—he was only being considerate. I'm sure he must be in a hurry to get back to the station. The people there are certain to be looking for him.'

She saw her cousin and the freighter exchange a look. Nate Archer shrugged and dropped his hand away from his gun, and Vinnie decided then that the unsuspecting young fellow on the seat beside her was to be spared. She had to be grateful for that, at least.

Wes Boyd held up his arms to her and said, 'Let me help you down.' Numbly, unprotesting, she let him lift her from the wagon; and when her feet touched the ground she had to clutch his arm to keep her knees from giving way. Wes dug a gold coin from his pocket and spun it up to Hickok. 'That's for your trouble,' he said with patronizing coolness. 'We won't keep you any longer.'

The young fellow nodded, put the money away and lifted the reins. Nate Archer had already removed Vinnie's carpetbag from behind the seat. Hickok looked again at Vinnie. 'Glad to of been a help, ma'am.' She nodded, unable to speak. They waited as he yelled at the horses, brought them around in a tight circle. After that he was rolling back the way they had come, oblivious to the peril he left behind him; and as she watched him go, Vinnie felt her cousin's hand close, hard, upon her arm.

She forced herself to raise her eyes to his, and saw the savage fury that twisted his face. 'All right, you little bitch!' he gritted. 'What are you trying to do to me?'

CHAPTER FOURTEEN

The blackest moment in Dan Rawley's life came when he saw Wes Boyd rounding the wagon tailgate, Vinnie Owen stumbling along beside him, his grip tight upon her arm. Dan stood with his back against one of the big wheels, blood drying on his mouth where one of Cap Shulte's heavy fists had smashed him. His arms were beginning to ache from being held shoulder-high; so did the muscles of his belly, tightened into knots with the momentary expectation of a bullet from Shulte's gun.

He was still stunned by the suddenness with which these men had struck the encamped wagons—splashing their horses across the stream, guns already drawn to fall upon the crew before anyone quite realized what was happening. Dimly, he judged Cap Shulte must have been given clear orders that, for whatever reason, Dan Rawley was to be kept alive. Given his own way, Shulte would far rather have seen him dead.

Now Vinnie Owen's cheeks were white as she stared at his bloody face and at Hobie

Drake sitting on the ground with his head hanging and groggy still from a blow from a gun barrel. She tried in vain to pull free from her cousin's hand. 'Dan!' she cried. 'They've hurt you!'

'Oh, hell!' Cap Shulte showed his teeth in a mocking grin. 'These two ain't even found out what hurtin' is, yet!'

Dan ignored the threat and the gun leveled at his middle. He stammered a question which Wes Boyd answered for him: 'She found out some way what we had in mind, Rawley. She went to Leavenworth and took the stage to try and overtake us. Can you imagine that?'

'I wanted to warn you!' Vinnie said, choking on a sob. 'I almost made it, too! Oh, Dan . . .'

Tears shone in her eyes as she stood helpless in her cousin's grasp. She looked badly rumpled from her ordeal on the stagecoach; she had lost her hat and her mass of taffy-colored hair had come unpinned. Yet to Dan Rawley she had never looked lovelier, and his heart sank within him. 'What are you going to do with her?' he demanded harshly, but Wes Boyd only scowled. It occurred to Dan that, in the face of this unexpected turn of events, he was clearly at a loss.

Nate Archer appeared, carrying Vinnie's carpetbag. He set the bag down and straightened, rubbing his palms nervously along the legs of his trousers—as hard as it was to believe it, from the way the others deferred to him, this inconsequential little man must actually be the leader and the brains behind everything that was happening. He spoke to the girl now.

'Have you eaten?'

She stared, incredulous. 'Do you think I could eat!'

'I think you'd better try,' the bald-headed man said crisply, 'while you have a chance.' And he gave one of Shulte's crew orders to fetch her a plate of food from over at the fire, where Dan Rawley's teamsters stood about in a sullen group under the watchful eyes and guns of their captors. As this was being done, Nate Archer turned for a cold look at Hobie Drake. In his most brusk, officious manner he asked Shulte, 'How's this one doing?'

The Dutchman snorted. 'A skull as thick as his—it ain't been more than dented.'

'Keep a close eye on him.' The gambler, Vern Merrick, stood leaning against the wagonbox with his arms folded and a look of bored disinterest on his raddled features, saying nothing. Archer told him, 'And I think you'd better keep an eye on Shulte. Don't let him get carried away again.' Merrick nodded shortly, and Archer turned again to Dan Rawley.

It must have been the black look on the latter's face that prompted Archer to slide the Navy Colt from his holster—he handled it awkwardly enough, but Dan knew that a gun in inexperienced and nervous hands could be doubly dangerous. The freighter's sunburned cheeks shone with sweat. He looked at Wes Boyd.

'Looks to me,' he said gruffly, 'the three of us are due for a little talk—right now. Let's walk over here by the creek.'

It was no more than a few steps, enough to give them privacy. Nate Archer moved with the spraddled stiffness of one made saddlesore by unaccustomed hours on horseback. He called a halt in the flickering shadow of some young cottonwoods, and Wes Boyd put one boot up on a fallen log and leaned forearm on knee while he stared moodily at the water. The murmur of the brook, and the whistling of a meadowlark out in the long grass beyond, seemed the only sounds in the whole vast sun-filled prairie.

Dan Rawley said coldly, 'Can I take my hands down?'

Archer flushed. 'Of course. We don't want to get rough with anyone, Daniel.'

'I'm glad to hear that,' he said wryly, as he lowered his arms and flexed the ache out of them. 'I was sort of wondering—the way you came busting down on us with your crew, and took my wagons away from me. And nearly broke Hobie Drake's skull.'

'That was Shulte,' the freighter insisted. 'And anyway, I hope it will be a warning. If you force us to, we can get very rough indeed. But if you show you're willing to cooperate—'

'How?' His temper threatened to slip its controls. 'Just what the devil more do you want from me? You've already taken my outfit. You've got the whip hand.'

'I'm glad you realize that. Just the same, Daniel—for old times' sake if nothing else— I'd like us to be able to work something out. We used to have our differences, while you were on my payroll, but I never denied that you were as good a wagon boss as any on the Trail. Cap Shulte can do the job, after a fashion; still, I'd like it a lot better if you'd only be willing to go along with us, and take these wagons where we tell you. I'd like it well enough that I'd be in favor of cutting you in for a share—probably even more than what Owen and his friends intend paying.'

Dan managed to keep his temper under control. 'And supposing I say no?'

'Then you're only being a fool!' Nate Archer retorted. 'You must see we've gone too far now to turn back. The girl complicates matters but doesn't change anything. What happens to her—and to your friend Hobie Drake, and to these teamsters of yours—I'm afraid all of it depends on whether you're willing to act sensibly.'

It was almost beyond belief, that he should be standing here and listening to this talk from such a trivial and unimportant creature as Nate Archer. The man was sweating again, but the look in his eyes and the gun in his hand were proof enough that he meant exactly what he said. Dan turned to Wes Boyd. 'You're really in this, too? All the way?'

But Boyd wouldn't look at him. He was kicking loose bark from the log, his head down, his eyes on what his boot was doing; he had the look of someone who has sealed himself off from logic and persuasion. Looking again at Archer, Dan suggested coldly, 'So, I do what you want. What happens to us then?'

'Why, that will have to be worked out, of course. But you don't have to worry—you'll all be treated fairly. Believe me, none of us wants to use uncivilized behavior. Unless, of course, we're forced to it.'

Dan Rawley took a slow breath. 'You don't give me much choice, do you?' he muttered grimly, and saw Nate Archer begin to grin with satisfaction and relief.

*   *   *

Cap Shulte took it worse than hard, when it came his turn to hear what had been agreed on. The news widened his eyes and bunched his cheek muscles, and then the beet-red tide of blood flowed swiftly up across the planes of his face, clear to his hairline.

'I'm damned if you do this to me!' he roared. 'What did I come along for, if it wasn't to boss these wagons?'

'We brought you to follow orders,' Archer said crisply—showing rather more bravery than Dan would have expected, in face of the Navy Colt that Shulte held. 'After the way you nearly lost that train for Work & Mantley, I ain't too apt to depend on you at all. In fact, from what I heard, it was Rawley saved the day for you that time, by straightening out your crew for you and knocking some sense into that thick skull.'

Stung to unbearable fury, Cap Shulte swore, and suddenly the muzzle of the gun was lifting—straight at Dan Rawley. The latter counted himself as good as dead, in the moment he stared into the black hole and felt his heartbeat clog and falter. Then, when no one else made a move, it was the gambler—Vern Merrick—who stepped forward to catch Shulte's wrist and shove it down and away. Merrick said, 'You'll do as you're told!'

Dan was to wonder, afterward, what might have happened if Shulte had decided on defiance. With six armed followers looking directly to him for their orders, surely a single word could have overpowered Archer and Boyd and Merrick and taken complete control. But the word wasn't spoken, and the moment passed. As the big fellow merely stood, scowling and irresolute, Nate Archer flung his own command at the silent crew: 'We're burning daylight. Get these wagons hitched and let's roll, before the afternoon gets any

193

older.'

In the sudden burst of activity around them, Dan had a chance for a word with Hobie Drake. Hobie was on his feet, now, though still looking a little sick with the clubbing he'd taken from Shulte's gun barrel. Not far away, Vinnie Owen sat on an upturned keg, watching them, her face white and the plate of food in her lap almost untouched.

'You all right?' Dan asked his partner, anxiously.

'What do you care?' Hobie retorted. He added bitterly: 'You and me got nothing to say!'

In pure astonishment, Dan saw the contempt peering at him from Hobie's brooding stare. Hobie's fists were knotted, hard, as though it took an effort to keep them at his sides. 'By God, I know how big a dollar looks to you but I never thought you'd reached this point. I never thought you'd throw in with them!'

Dan Rawley found himself shaking his head, trying to protest: 'You don't understand!' But the words died in his throat as Hobie spat, deliberately just missing the toe of his partner's boot. Abruptly, he turned his back in a manner that made it clear he wanted to hear nothing more that Dan might say.

Dan could only watch him walk away. He thought he was almost able to feel the shock and distress in Vinnie's eyes, and her anxious face . . .

In seizing this shipment, Cap Shulte had taken the precaution of ordering every teamster and wagon searched, every weapon confiscated and thrown into the creek. This caused some grumbling, but bullwhackers as a breed were no more inclined to be heroes than any other man. Having no personal stake in a struggle for possession of the cargo they had been hired to deliver, it was natural enough they should wait and take their cue from Dan Rawley. When it became clear he had reached some kind of agreement with their captors, the crew followed suit and took their orders as though nothing that had happened made any difference.

Even so, Shulte took no chances. Through the long afternoon, as the stolen wagons rolled ponderously forward, he and his riders kept a careful watch, patrolling the length of the captured train with rifles across knees and pistols ready in belt holsters. For his own part, Archer never let Dan Rawley for long out of his sight. Dan was aware of him, constantly hovering—not interfering, but watching everything with a malevolence that plainly waited for his enemy to make a misstep. His presence and the weight of his stare were enough to touch Dan with a cold chill.

Ironically enough, the haul was going well. This many days out of Bellport, things had shaken down to a comfortable routine. The stock was in good shape, and the specially constructed rigs were standing up to the job they had been built for. As he pulled up at the head of the train to watch one of the giant boilers go by him, its double length of bull-teams bowing heavy shoulders to the yoke, Dan couldn't help feeling a certain pride—even now, even after the disaster—in the job he and Hobie Drake had done in preparing for this haul, and in getting it on the road.

Now the train rolled under guard. And Hobie Drake lay trussed up in one of the wagons down the line, apparently convinced beyond argument that Dan Rawley was a traitor, hardly even any better than Wes Boyd himself. Hobie couldn't seem to get it into his skull that if Dan hadn't agreed to work with their captors, they would likely both be dead by now.

And, Vinnie . . .

He saw her now, dejected and alone on the seat of an approaching wagon. Their captors seemed bent on keeping them apart; up to now he hadn't had a chance to speak more than a dozen words to her. Suddenly a determination settled his jaw and, swinging the bay around, he rode over to fall in beside the high, turning wheel.

'Are you all right?' he asked. She looked at him. Her lips moved, turned heavy with despair and no sound came after them. Her eyes swam with tears and wavered from his own.

Dan didn't know if the bullwhacker, plodding beside his wheel team on the wagon's far side, could hear him above the slam and creak of the heavy timbers. He must be careful, for fear that the wrong words could somehow reach the ears of their enemies. And yet, he had to speak. 'Vinnie!' he exclaimed. 'Surely you know I *have* to do what I'm doing? If I refused, they'd just manage without me.'

It was hard to tell if his words even registered. Her eyes were vacant with shock and fatigue. She shook her head vaguely, looking at some point on the horizon. 'I don't know,' she said. 'I don't—'

Somebody spoke Dan's name, harshly. He turned in the saddle, and Nate Archer and Cap Shulte were pulling in on either side of him, bracketing the bay with their horses. Shulte's heavy face was gloating, dangerous. Archer's sweating cheeks glistened as he said, 'I think you better stay away from the girl, Daniel. I don't like you talking to her. It makes me uneasy.'

'Does it?' His words were as flat as the line of his lips.

The sunburnt face glowed with heightened color. 'I said before,' Archer told him, his voice rising, 'for old times' sake, I don't want to have to do anything bad to you. But, we can't afford to just automatically trust you— and you can't afford to do anything that might

197

rouse our suspicion. You understand?'

Dan looked at him for a long moment, flicked the barest glance at Shulte. The wagon had already moved ahead, taking Vinnie with it. Without a word, Dan simply backed his horse from between the others and kicked it into a lope, moving in the opposite direction along the slowly moving string of wagons. He could all but feel the eyes of the two men, staring after him.

* * *

Tied hand and foot, and thrown into the back of a wagon that was loaded to the bows with massive crates of machinery parts, Hobie Drake had been having a miserable time of it. There was no way, twist and turn though he might, that he could make himself comfortable, or ease at all the hard jounce and slam that seemed enough to grind his flesh to mincemeat. To add to that, the smear of sunlight on canvas concentrated its heat in this narrow space of dead air beneath the tight-drawn wagon tarp, sucking the sweat from him and filling him with panicky thoughts of suffocation. For a while he had yelled and cursed and fought at his bonds; finally worn out, he had lapsed into a kind of delirious torpor, no longer even aware of time at all.

It was the cessation of movement that finally brought him out of this, to the unbelievable relief of complete stillness. Men were moving about. Lying there, Hobie Drake could hear the scrape of footsteps, the rumble of talk. He lifted his head and tried to cry out. His throat and mouth and lips were parched and dry as cotton; nobody could have heard the hoarse croak that was all he managed. But presently someone came and began working at the lashings of the wagon cover. The canvas slid back; it let a tide of fresh air pour in at him, with a touch that felt ice-cold as it penetrated his sweat-soaked clothing. A voice said, 'All right, you! Come out of there.'

Blinking in the light, he saw that the short spring evening was settling over the plains. Camp had been made. The big wagons were circled, and men were busy outspanning and leading their teams to water and graze. A couple of Shulte's men stood staring in at Hobie. With them, he saw his particular enemy—Vern Merrick—who he knew had never forgiven him for that night at Milligan's when Hobie had exposed his tinhorn trickery to the whole crowd.

Sooner or later, Hobie thought as he looked at the sick and ravaged face, I suppose this man is going to kill me!

The order was repeated, with dangerous impatience. Though his ankles were tied and his hands lashed behind his back, no one made a move to help him and Hobie gathered that he was going to have to get out of that wagon under his own power. When he tried to move, every cramped and pounded muscle protested. Somehow he managed to roll and hitch himself off the crate, and drop his boots onto the tailgate. Braced there, he slid to a sitting position and was trying to figure a way to manuever himself to the ground, when Vern Merrick simply reached up, grabbed him by the waistband and pulled him down. Powerless to catch himself, Hobie fell; he landed heavily on his face and chest.

Somebody laughed as though he thought that was funny as hell. A boot toe nudged Hobie. Merrick's voice said, 'On your feet. Quit taking all day!'

Dazed as he was, he tried gamely, but without the use of his hands he couldn't seem to manage. On the second attempt, he was able to push himself precariously to his knees. As he was wondering how he would proceed from there, he heard a horse brought to a stand and a new voice demanded sharply, 'What's going on here?'

Hobie lifted his head with an effort. His eyes traveled up the legs of the bay horse, on up to Dan Rawley seated in the saddle. Their eyes met and held for a moment; then Dan's head lifted and he put his hard stare on Hobie's tormentors. 'Just what do you think you're doing to him?'

These three were armed, and Dan was not. Even Merrick, who seemed to prefer relying

200

on his pocket derringer, had strapped on a belt and holster that looked awkwardly out of place on him. He touched the handle of the revolver now and said, in a mean voice, 'Stay out of this.'

Dan ignored the warning. Deliberately swinging from the saddle, he hooked a hand under Hobie's arm and, with an effort, hauled the big fellow to his feet. 'If I know of this man being treated like this again,' he said sternly, 'any deal I ever made with you people is off. Now, somebody give me a knife so I can cut him loose.'

No one moved. But Hobie Drake, with the taste of blood and dirt on his tongue, looked at this partner of his who had sold out to the enemy—and who had spent these past hours comfortably in the saddle, without a mark on him. Contrast with his own bruised and sorry state drew a snarl from Hobie and he jerked away from Dan's touch so violently that, trussed up as he was, only the wagon tailgate catching his shoulders saved him from another tumble. Bitterly he said, 'Don't do me no favors, Rawley. Far as I'm concerned you can go straight to hell!'

Dan Rawley snatched his hand back as though he'd been stung. He met Hobie's furious stare; his own face lost its color and then turned mottled as the blood rushed into it. Hobie could see he was trying to find speech, and then his mouth set hard and the muscles knotted along his jaw. He swung away, his shoulders stiffly straight, and caught up the reins and walked off without another word or look, the bay trailing.

Hobie watched him go, unrelenting in the bitter anger that had had an interminable afternoon to grow and rankle.

Later he sat in brooding solitude, his back to one of the big wagon wheels, tied there. The sounds of the wagon camp carried thinly across the empty wastes. The smoke of two large fires, and the odor of cooking, made his stomach rumble. Hobie wondered bitterly if Dan and his new friends intended to feed him, or let him starve.

He didn't know why they didn't just knock him in the head and get it over with. He was a dead weight on their hands and an embarrassment to his former partner— assuming there was still some vestige of shame or decency left in Dan Rawley. Or maybe Dan thought that, in time, he'd come around and agree to throw in with their captors.

Damned if he'd ever do it—not after they'd spilled enough to make it clear just where this stolen mill was going. To the dirty Secessionists, by God! To the Southern traitors who were even now firing on the Stars and Stripes at Fort Sumter!

Still, the smell of frying pork and boiling beans and coffee was pretty overpowering. He sat there listening to his stomach growl, and watched supper being prepared at the nearer of the two fires. Vinnie Owen was helping with the cooking—she couldn't be blamed for that, she had to eat too. Hobie could see her moving about, the hem of her traveling dress tucked up out of her way, her face grave and her manner unapproachable. She spoke to no one, except in monosyllables and only when she had to. Once Hobie had seen Dan Rawley come to her, to stand awkwardly about for a moment—trying to argue with her, it looked like, and being wholly ignored until at last he shook his head and walked away again.

What did he expect from Frank Owen's daughter? After what he had done?

Now as Hobie watched, she filled a tin plate with food and poured a cup of coffee, and spoke to Cap Shulte who was just then passing. Cap stopped to face her in the fireglow; they seemed to debate something. The big Dutchman rubbed a fist across his jaw, then shrugged. Together they approached the place where Hobie sat with his ankles bound, and both arms raised and lashed to spokes of the wagon wheel at the level of his ears. 'All right, you!' Cap Shulte told him. 'The lady says you got to eat, so I'm cutting one hand free so's you can manage. But don't make any mistakes—or try anything funny. You hear me?'

'That food talks louder than you do,' Hobie grunted. 'Go ahead.'

203

Shulte worked at the rawhide lashing that held the prisoner's right wrist to the wheel. He stepped back alert and suspicious, as Hobie lowered his arm, grimacing a little as he flexed the fingers to send blood tingling back into them. Then Vinnie came forward, offering the plate of steaming food. He reached—and nearly dropped it.

Underneath the plate, his fingers touched a wooden handle, and sharp steel; his glance shot to meet the girl's, saw her answering, warning look. And, carefully expressionless, he closed his fingers upon the haft of the knife which she had somehow managed to steal, and hide, and slip to him.

CHAPTER FIFTEEN

It was a quiet evening. The steady plains wind had ceased at day's end, and the low sun put its spears of light through the drift of dust and layered smoke from the fires. Dan Rawley moved through the camp, stony-faced and unapproachable, giving orders mechanically as he oversaw the unyoking of the teams and the preparations for night security. Behind a cold facade, he was actually nursing the deep hurt of his rebuff by Hobie Drake. And in this near-savage mood, he all at once found himself confronted by Wes Boyd, face to face.

Boyd stood beside one of the big wagons, a plate of food in his hands and a steaming cup of coffee set on a timber at his elbow. He halted a spoonful of beans half way to his mouth and the two men eyed one another, through a hostile and wary silence. Dan was certain that Boyd had been deliberately keeping out of his way. He felt somehow there must be a bad conscience at work; the thought prompted him now to say quietly, 'How about it, Boyd? Are you happy about everything?'

Anger gathered in the darkly bearded face, and some other emotion that was harder to read. Boyd dropped his spoon back into the plate; his hand trembled slightly. He said, 'Leave me alone, Rawley.'

'What reason have you got to beef?' Dan retorted coldly. 'So far, everything's gone pretty much the way you and your friends had it planned. You should be feeling good, about now.'

The other man's voice shook. 'Damn you, I don't need your sarcasm!'

'You rather I said right out what I think?' Dan exclaimed, reckless temper roughening his tongue. 'The Owens certainly deserve better than this! Vinnie—your own cousin . . . And I don't see how even you could choose this way to repay all that Frank has done for you!'

Boyd swore at him and a convulsive movement of his elbow struck the tin cup and knocked it flying, to trail a brown streak of coffee as it clattered over the trampled earth. 'I'm warning you, Rawley!' he cried. 'Lay off!'

'Or what?' Dan retorted 'Or just exactly what, mister?'

The two men stood and glared, the sparks almost visibly crackling between them. But Dan Rawley's challenge never did get a direct answer; for just then, excitement broke out somewhere at the other side of the compound: a single cry, and after that a burst of shouting, and mingling with it the first startling gunshot.

Nerves that had been stretched too tight leaped convulsively. As Dan jerked around for a look, the low sun stabbed in between a couple of the parked wagons and nearly blinded him. Even when he ducked his head and lifted a shielding hand, he could see little enough. But behind the drift of golden dust and wood smoke, men were yelling. Once again a pistol shot sounded, then a pair almost together.

Wes Boyd's tin plate fell with a clatter and, glancing quickly, Dan saw the long-barreled gun pointed awkwardly in his direction. Boyd warned hoarsely, 'Whatever's going on, you stay out of it! Stand where you are! You hear me?'

Dan looked at the gun, and at the man who held it, and he made his decision. 'Go to hell!' he retorted, and deliberately turned and walked away.

He didn't think Wes Boyd had the nerve to shoot anyone in the back, though he couldn't be certain; the muscles across his shoulders knotted hard in apprehension. Yet he kept on, without faltering, and heard no further challenge—no sound at all, behind him. By degrees he could allow himself to breathe again.

More shooting, beyond that gilded screen of dust. Dan broke into a run. He saw a couple of Cap Shulte's guards hurrying in the same direction, but nobody seemed to be thinking of Dan Rawley just then and no one interfered with him. Then, shouldering aside a teamster who blundered into his path, he had his first clear glimpse of what was happening.

It was Hobie Drake—loose, by God, and on the warpath!

Dan Rawley halted, stunned. He could only guess that Hobie must have laid hands on a knife some way, for the severed rawhide thongs dangled at his wrists and the knife lay yonder where he'd dropped it, its blade brightly red. There too was one of Shulte's guards, swearing and rolling in the dirt and clutching at a leg with both hands, while blood flowed and soaked into the cloth of his trousers. It must have been he who'd got in the way of the knife blade; so, obviously, it was with the gun taken from his empty holster that Hobie was defending himself now.

Having used up a couple of bullets in an

attempt to discourage his enemies as they came at him from every part of the wagon circle, Hobie was trying to find shelter. The nearest of any kind was the underrigging of one of the big wagons; he was making for that—scurrying in a bent-over, crab-wise run, as though to make a smaller target. And Dan had time to think: Hobie, you stubborn fool! You wouldn't trust your own partner—so you'll throw your life away going it alone!

Suddenly he thought his heart had stopped; he saw his friend falter, thought certain he had been hit, then decided Hobie's boot had merely slipped in the grass. But at the same moment, one of Shulte's men braked to a halt a yard or so in front of Dan Rawley, and stood to take deliberate aim. Dan could actually look past his shoulder and along his arm as he lined up his shot. At that range, it could hardly miss. He was sure Hobie didn't see the danger; his throat closed tight on the warning yell he wanted to get out and couldn't.

Everything seemed to go into a queer sort of slow motion then.

Dan saw his own arm reaching, felt the lurch and strain of his leg muscles driving him forward; yet he had no sense of movement and his impressions, though sharply vivid, appeared separate and disjointed. He heard the explosion, almost in his face. Through the spurt of white smoke he had a glimpse of Hobie Drake looking as though he had frozen, grotesquely, in the instant the bullet hit. And he carried that picture with him as he barreled into the man who held the gun.

With strange detachment, he watched the man's head start to turn. His own fist seemed to hang motionless before it struck solidly, just behind the ear. Bone and tendon jarred his knuckles. Though Dan pulled his arm back and chopped him again, the man was already folding. The gun popped out of his fingers; still bothered by that odd derangement of the sense of time, Dan almost thought he could reach and pluck it from mid-air.

But this was mere illusion, of course. Vaguely, he realized his own momentum had carried him too far, and that the man who was crumpling in front of him had tripped him up. He went down and over him, stabbing out with both hands in an effort to catch himself. After that Dan was on the ground and there was the gun, lying directly in front of him.

As he reached for it, Dan looked up and was alarmed to discover Vinnie Owen standing all alone, quite near him, both palms pressed to her cheeks while she stared at him in helpless terror. She was completely vulnerable to flying bullets—Dan shouted at her to get back, to get down, but doubted if she even heard. For his own part he was anxious to learn the true situation with Hobie Drake; but there was no time now for that either, because Cap Shulte was coming toward him across the trampled grass with a Navy Colt in his fist.

Lying there, on one elbow, Dan caught up the gun and hurriedly fired. There was nothing—only the snap of the pin striking a defective cap. He broke into a sweat, at that, and fought the hammer-spur to bring it into firing position again. The clammy moisture caused his thumb to slip. By this time, Shulte was almost on top of him, charging out of the sunset glare and into the shadow of the big wagon that loomed somewhere in back of Dan. The gun muzzle in Shulte's hand blossomed with fire. A bullet, narrowly missing, clanged like an anvil strike as it went on to slam into a heavy tire-rim.

Then Dan tried the trigger again, and this time his shot was good. The gun kicked against his sweating palm. Hit in the chest, Shulte was stopped in mid-stride and, with horror and fascination, Dan watched him fall.

When he remembered to breathe, he nearly choked on the rawness of burnt powder. The shouting had quit. Suddenly it was so quiet the crackling of the fire could be clearly heard, and the lonely whistle of a meadowlark somewhere out in the grass. Dan got slowly to his feet, clutching the smoking gun and watching Cap Shulte to make certain the man was really dead. Warily, he took a step toward him and then another. And abruptly stiffened.

Vern Merrick's voice spoke behind him: 'You'll stop right where you are, friend, and you'll drop the gun. The hand is run out for you . . .'

No one moved at all. Teamsters and guards alike stood watching, immobile, to see what Dan Rawley would do. The man he'd knocked down and disarmed was on his feet again, with a hand pressed to his swelling jaw, staring dumbly. Even the victim of Hobie Drake's knife thrust, still huddled in the dirt, seemed more concerned with what was happening just now than he was with his own skewered leg. Feeling all these eyes on him, Dan slowly turned.

The muzzle of Vern Merrick's Colt revolver loomed like the bore of a cannon.

Nate Archer stood at his elbow, but Archer's gun hadn't left its holster. Archer looked a little ill. Dan could see his head shaking slightly, as with a tic. But his companion's controls were steady enough. Now Merrick reminded his prisoner, harshly, 'You still haven't got rid of the gun . . .'

Dan Rawley looked down at it. He was conscious of Vinnie staring at him, pale and frightened and disheveled. He lifted his shoulders, and with a hopeless gesture tossed the gun aside.

'Looks like you win,' he told his captors.

Nate Archer found his voice now—he spoke accusingly, as though a great injustice had been done to him: 'Daniel, we had an agreement. You gave your word!'

'You didn't keep yours,' Dan reminded him bitterly. 'After promising me Hobie Drake was to be treated halfway decently—not trussed up like a hog and thrown in a wagon. And now, I suppose you've killed him!'

Over there in a shadow of the wagon he could see his friend's body, lying crumpled and completely motionless. Archer made an impatient gesture. 'It's too bad about Drake— but he was a stubborn fool, after all, who wouldn't listen to reason. Don't you be making the same mistake, Daniel!'

Vern Merrick said, 'A little late for that. He's already made his mistake!'

That remark brought a startled look from Archer. 'What do you mean?'

'I think you know what I mean, as well as I do!'

'No!' Nate Archer's eyes widened in alarm; the word all but exploded from him. 'You're not to kill him! I won't have that. We never planned on any killing. There mustn't be any more.'

'There's going to be one more,' the gambler retorted, flatly. 'After all this, how can we risk keeping him alive?'

Stammering, the other protested. 'But— we've already lost Shulte. Who will it leave us to boss these wagons?'

'Why, it looks like *you* might have to tackle it, Nate.' The gambler let an edge of contempt into his voice. 'Seems I've been hearing you call yourself a freighter. Here's a fine chance for you to show just how much use you can be to this enterprise—if any. Because I'll tell you right now, I'm taking no more chances with your friend Rawley! None at all!'

He meant it. From the mere tone of his voice, Dan knew then that death was exactly as close as the pressure of Merrick's finger on the trigger, and the knowledge put a brassy taste of fear in his mouth. Determined to be as much of a man as Hobie Drake had been, he lifted his head higher and forced himself to meet the cold eyes in that unhealthy ravaged face.

Vinnie Owen gave a sudden, whimpering cry. Before anyone could have guessed what she was up to, in spite of her terror she had run forward to throw herself at the gambler and was fighting him with all her strength, tearing at his arm with both hands as she tried to dislodge his grip on the gun. Vern Merrick swore roundly. A single jerk freed his arm. Beside himself with rage, the man turned on her and the opened fingers of one hand lashed right across the girl's face. She was flung aside and, tangling in her skirts, went down in a sprawl.

The gambler staggered. As the flat crack of a single gunshot beat itself to echoes, Vern Merrick's shoulder hunched, his head dropped forward, and as though a tremendous force had rammed him in the middle, he began to fold. He looked around him once; then his knees buckled under him. He dropped his Colt revolver, and fell on it as Wes Boyd walked up with the pistol in his hand still dribbling smoke.

Boyd stared, white and shaken, at the man he had killed. He looked at Nate Archer, and at Dan who was already hurrying to help Vinnie to her feet. 'Is she hurt?'

Dan shook his head. He slipped an arm around the girl and she put her face into the hollow of his shoulder and clung to him, trembling. Boyd shuddered and ran the palm of a hand down across his bearded cheeks and mouth. 'Thank God for that, at least!' he muttered. 'I don't know Rawley. Perhaps you were right, and I don't really amount to much. Perhaps it was the tongue-lashing you gave me. But, this was something I just couldn't have stood for!'

Nate Archer tore his eyes away from the man who lay dead at his feet. 'Do you realize what you've done?'

'Don't say it!' Boyd cut him off savagely. 'Don't say one thing to me, Archer!' The muzzle of the gun in his hand shifted suddenly, and settled directly on the freighter's narrow chest. Nate Archer sucked in his breath and a pasty pallor began to spread beneath the sunburn, turning his face oddly mottled.

'This little adventure of yours is finished,' Wes Boyd told him. 'I'm giving Rawley back his wagons . . .'

*   *   *

Later, Dan Rawley would always be a little
unsure about this whole, bewildering change
of circumstances, but he wasn't too confused
to take advantage of it. Once satisfied that
Vinnie was unhurt, he lost no time shoving
Nate Archer's coattail aside and lifting the gun
from his holster. Of Cap Shulte's guards only
four remained to be disarmed, and finding
themselves leaderless had taken the fight out
of them. They made no resistance when Dan
gave his teamsters orders to lift their weapons.
When the one with the knife wound in his leg
had been taken care of, it seemed to him
probably safe enough for the lot of them to be
given their horses and turned loose.

Dan had more urgent business. He would
have turned away, but he halted impatiently as
Wes Boyd said, 'One minute, Rawley! To get
the record straight, I want you to know why it
was they were able to put the hooks into me in
the first place. The reason is in Nate Archer's
pocket.'

The freighter made a convulsive move to
prevent him, but the other man knocked his
hand aside and from inside his coat removed a
sheaf of papers. Dan, frowning, took them and
ran a thumb across their edges. He looked at
Boyd sharply. 'Gambling notes . . . I guess I

215

understand.'

Boyd said gruffly, 'I don't ask any special treatment. I was in the thing, right along with the rest of them. I don't know—I might even have gone through with it.'

'But you didn't,' Dan pointed out. 'This is something you'll have to settle with your uncle, but at least you've got my thanks. As for these things—' Dan shrugged, and calmly tore the notes in two and then again. 'You must have known they had no standing, except as a matter of honor. I don't imagine friend Archer will be trying to collect on them now!'

Turning on his heel he swung away, pausing long enough to drop the worthless gambling notes into the fire—the torn scraps took flame and were carried high and scattered on the updraft, as he walked on through the gathering dusk to the place where Vinnie was already on her knees beside Hobie Drake.

Hobie was conscious. He was half-sprawled, half-sitting with his shoulders against a big wheel, and Vinnie had the bloody shirt sleeve ripped away from the bullet gouge along the meat of his left upper arm. 'It ain't too bad, actually,' he said when he saw Dan leaning over him; but his face was white and his voice as shaky. 'Somehow it just seemed to knock the sauce out of me.'

'You're going to be all right,' Dan said after a brief examination. 'It's quit bleeding. Just take it easy while I fetch the first aid box.'

216

But Hobie shook his head. 'That ain't what hurts the worst,' he exclaimed. 'It's knowing I been acting like all kinds of a damned fool. Dan, I'm sorry. More than that—I'm ashamed!'

'Forget it,' Dan told him. 'You couldn't have helped but wonder what I thought I was up to. I'd have had no call to blame you.'

His partner caught at his sleeve. 'No! I mean this! Next time I start behaving funny, you got to promise you'll whop me one and knock some sense in my skull! You've heard the news, about Fort Sumter. Sure looks like this poor old country of ours may have one helluva big fight ahead of it. And, damn it, at a time like that, folks such as you and me have got no business fighting amongst ourselves!'

Dan looked at his friend a long moment, and then at Vinnie's grave and troubled face. Slowly he nodded.

'You're absolutely right,' he agreed, soberly. 'That's a thing worth remembering. Let's hope we never forget it.'